# Loyalty Ain't Promised

Lock Down Publications and Ca$h
Presents

# Loyalty Ain't Promised

A Novel by *Keith Williams*

**Lock Down Publications**
P.O. Box 870494
Mesquite, Tx 75187

**Lock Down Publications**
**Like our page on Facebook: Lock Down Publications @**
www.facebook.com/lockdownpublications.ldp
Cover design and layout by: **Dynasty Cover Me**
Book interior design by: **Shawn Walker**
Edited by: **Kiera Northington**

# Stay Connected with Us!

Text **LOCKDOWN** to 22828 to stay up-to-date with new releases, sneak peaks, contests and more...

Thank you!

# Submission Guideline.

Submit the first three chapters of your completed manuscript to ldpsubmissions@gmail.com, subject line: Your book's title. The manuscript must be in a .doc file and sent as an attachment. Document should be in Times New Roman, double spaced and in size 12 font. Also, provide your synopsis and full contact information. If sending multiple submissions, they must each be in a separate email.

Have a story but no way to send it electronically? You can still submit to LDP/Ca$h Presents. Send in the first three chapters, written or typed, of your completed manuscript to:

LDP: Submissions Dept
P.O. Box 870494
Mesquite, Tx 75187

*DO NOT send original manuscript. Must be a duplicate.*

Provide your synopsis and a cover letter containing your full contact information.

Thanks for considering LDP and Ca$h Presents.

Keith Williams

# Chapter One
## Mahogany

"Times like this got a bitch feeling like saying fuck the world," I said to myself as I weaved through traffic and cursed every man in the world who's ever cheated.

Standing a petite five foot five, with cream-colored skin, money-green eyes and six solid gold caps gracing the bottom row of my teeth. I was a five-star bitch, and everybody in the city of Deland, Florida, knew I was Beyoncé's motivation for making the song, "Flawless."

I was on my way home to confront my boyfriend, a sexy young nigga who stood a solid six foot even, with smooth skin the color of a Twix candy bar, and enough waves in his head to make any woman get seasick. He went by the name of Supreme, which he adopted from the streets when he was a fourteen-year-old teenager, because he had the ambition of a man who was trying to reach a million.

I had just called his cellphone and some woman answered, talking about, stay away from her man. I was shocked because I knew how Supreme was about people touching his phone, so for a bitch to be answering it, he had to be slipping on his pimpin' and now I'm about to catch him.

I drove thirty minutes to our two-story suburban home in Debary and every five minutes, something foul came out of my mouth. I hated him at the moment, because he was giving them bitches in the streets a reason to laugh in my face. Shit, they were getting the dick more than I was.

I finally pulled into the driveway, parked my pearl white six-series Beamer next to his black Lexis coupe, and hopped out. I walked so fast trying to get to the front door that I almost I broke the heel on my designer pumps and fell face first on the ground. I was heated.

*Boom, Boom, Boom, Boom*

"Supreme, open this door right now!" I yelled at the top of my lungs as I tried to beat the door down. I did this for five whole minutes and got no answer, until I finally thought to try the doorknob. I turned it and to my surprise, the door opened, making me look like the backside of a donkey. At least, that's how I felt. "Supreme!" I yelled again as I walked through the house, checking every closed door in my path. When I got to our room and opened the door, his eyes were glued to the security monitors watching my every move, from the time I'd pulled into the driveway. "Where that bitch at? I hope she still here," I shouted, roaming the whole room with my eyes.

"Baby, what are you talking about? Why are you trippin'?" Supreme responded, slightly laughing.

"Oh, so this shit is funny to you?" I stopped in the middle of my sentence and shifted my head to the left once I saw movement out of my peripheral vision. "Who the hell is that?" I asked as I walked towards our bed, seeing the outline of a body. The closer I got, the more anxious I became, because I knew I had finally caught him. I pulled the blanket back and to my surprise, there in the bed was Ja'mya, Supreme's little sister.

"Who you thought you was gone see, another woman?" Supreme asked and smiled at the expression that was left on my face. I wanted to ask him who the female was that answered his cellphone, but now that I think about it, it had to be Ja'mya's young ass playing with me. I was embarrassed now, because for the second time today, I was looking like the backside of a donkey.

"Bae, you gotta quit being so tough, and let me be the boss sometimes," he said, walking up to me and wrapping his hands around my waist. I slightly laughed, then forced him to stare into my piercing green eyes.

"You turned me into your gangsta bitch. I didn't choose this lifestyle. You chose it for me. And besides, what other bitch do you trust to take charge while dealing with your connect and transporting your dope for you?"

He hesitated for a second like he was deep in thought, and then he kissed me with so much passion that my nipples poked him in the chest, forcing him to take a step backwards.

"That's what I'm talking about," he said excitedly after coating his thick lips with saliva. He then continued kissing me while easing his right hand up my dress, and into my womanhood.

"Mmmm," I moaned and closed my eyes as my muscles squeezed his fingers. I was getting so wet from his magic touch that my juices started running down my legs, and within seconds, I was erupting like a volcano. After my body calmed down from going into overdrive, I opened my eyes to find Ja'mya staring me straight in the face, while Supreme sucked his fingers like he was tasting a newly invented flavor. My whole face turned red, and I tried to get out of there quick as I could. I was ashamed another female saw my "O" face.

"Where you think you're going?" Supreme asked, grabbing hold of my arm before I could get too far.

"Baby, your sister was watching us," I responded with my head now deep into the nape of his neck. He smiled, then looked towards the bed and just like I said, Ja'mya was watching us like we were the newest show on BET.

"C'mon," he said, guiding me out the room and into the hall-way. Soon as he closed the door behind us, I hauled off and punched him in the chest hard as I could.

"Why did you do that, knowing your little sister was in there?" I asked, still feeling a little embarrassed.

"You telling me you didn't enjoy that?"

"That ain't the point."

"Well, what you complaining about then?" he asked, getting the last question in. And then he flashed that grin of his.

I wanted to bite off his lips. "I gotta go meet the connect and pick up your package in a little bit, so I can't stay."

"What!" He was clearly disappointed. His shaft was rock-hard and poking me in the stomach. "C'mon bae, you gone leave me like this?" He pointed down to his wood.

I stared in his face, astounded that he was so desperate. I knew niggas got whipped over the punany, but damn, not Supreme. "What's more important to you baby, money or pussy?" I asked.

"Money!"

"Well, act like it." I turned and walked out without looking back.

It was July 2018, and it felt like a heat wave had swept through. I was sweating heavily as I made my way to Atlanta, Georgia, in a 2002 Honda Accord that had no AC. I had an important meeting with Supreme's connect, Mr. Doe Boy Magic, concerning a more suitable price for the product.

Once, I reached the ATL, I pulled up to a club called Magic City and checked my surroundings. Things looked kosher, but I still strapped up. I grabbed my gun from the compartment between the seats, tucking it into my thigh-high, red bottom stilettos, before grabbing my MK duffle bag. I walked towards the entrance of the club like I was on the runway, because I knew somebody had to be watching me on the security camera. Like always, I was right and the beeping of the door indicating it had just been unlocked, proved it. I walked past the bouncer at the door and straight into Doe Boy's office. Being that my name was Mahogany, and Doe Boy wanted to fuck me so bad, he never let his men search me, because he couldn't stand seeing anybody's hands all over my body, females included.

"If it ain't the infamous Ms. Mahogany, then my eyes playing tricks on me. What's going on, baby?" Doe Boy asked, standing to his feet to greet me. Doe Boy was like the ultimate hustler of Atlanta, the brick mason. Even Big Meech respected his hustle game. Standing a solid six foot four, with chocolate skin, and strong features, Doe Boy was the man with the plan, that's why every female in Atlanta wanted to fuck him, and every nigga wanted to fuck with him.

"You know the only reason I come all the way up here is when it's about money," I responded, giving Doe Boy a hug and tossing the duffle bag on top of his desk.

"Yeah, I know, but tell me this. When are you going to stop fucking with that nigga Supreme, and fuck with a real baller? I can do way more for you than he can," Doe Boy started with his usual conversation about me leaving Supreme.

"I'm not with Supreme for what he can or can't do for me. It's all about loyalty with us, so long as it's there, I'ma be there," I said, taking a seat on his plush couch rather than the chair in front of his desk. He rushed to my side with two glasses of tequila, which he knew was my favorite, but I declined it. "Thanks, but no thanks. I don't drink when I'm on business," I said, watching him watch me. I broke our stare after about fifteen seconds and motioned towards the duffle bag on top of his desk. "That's two hundred and twenty thousand. Supreme is ready to up his shipment. He's already buying five at twenty-eight, he's willing to buy ten a week if you drop the price down to twenty-two thousand," I stated with confidence.

"I wish I had a woman like you. Supreme's a lucky man. I hope he knows that. I'll do it only because I like the way you demand what you want, and I like to see a woman try to help her man make it to the top," he responded. Doe Boy was really starting to get on my last nerve. I mean, I understand he wants me, but damn, how many ways you gotta tell a bitch that. The shit was getting me aggravated. He walked to his desk, grabbed the duffle bag, and poured all the money on top of it before passing me back my bag. "Throw him your keys," he said, pointing towards the bouncer standing at the door. I did what I was told and softly tossed my keys before turning my attention back to Doe Boy, who was in the process of placing stacks of bills in the safe under his desk.

"Doe Boy, what happened to your girlfriend, Tiffany? I haven't seen her in a while," I asked. He stopped what he was doing and looked up from under the desk with a stale face.

"I caught her cheating with one of my bouncers, so I had to let her go. I swear, I gave that girl anything she wanted, but I guess I wasn't laying the pipe to her good enough. Ain't that why y'all cheat on a nigga, right?" he responded. I don't know if he was making a statement or asking me a question, but I'm one of a kind, so you can't put me in the category with no bitch on this earth.

"First of all," I started, forcing him to stare into my green eyes. "Every woman that cheats have her own reason for doing so, so you can miss me with that *y'all* shit. And second, Mahogany will tell a nigga straight up that he needs to step his game up or I'm leaving if he's not satisfying me."

This time he broke our stare, turning his attention back to his money. I could tell he didn't like what I said, but fuck it, it is what it is. I said it just to piss him off anyway, because everybody in Atlanta knew Tiffany cheated on him because he couldn't fuck, and his dick was the size of a toddler's. At least, that's what the rumor was.

After about thirty minutes, the bouncer came back, nodded towards Doe Boy before handing me my keys. "Everything's taken care of, same time, same place next week," Doe Boy stated, reaching his arms out to give me a hug. I just stared at him like he had the Ebola virus before turning towards the door.

"I'm just kidding," I said, laughing at his facial expression, then giving him a big hug. He grabbed a handful of my ass with his big rough hand and lifted me up, so we were eye level with each other.

"You lucky I'ma gentleman or I would've been took this pussy." I just smirked at his comment, thinking, *how he talking about taking something when a bitch won't even feel anything, if he did try to penetrate me*? He put me back down and I walked towards the door, knowing he and his bouncer were staring at my ass as I left.

The six-hour drive back to Deland took about eight and had me more nervous than a woman who was headed to see her man in prison with four ounces of dope in her pussy. Two inmates had escaped from the Thomasville County Jail, so the sheriffs and state troopers were stopping and searching every vehicle that crossed the Florida-Georgia line.

I pulled up to Supreme's stash house on 23rd and 14th Street, and parallel parked next to a gray Magnum with spinning chrome rims. I knew it didn't belong to Supreme, so the first thing I did was hit his cellphone up. "Baby, where you at?" I asked soon as I heard his voice.

"I'm on my way right now."

"No! I didn't ask you that. I asked, where are you?" I repeated myself getting impatient. He answered this time, getting the hint by the tone of my voice that I was not in the mood for games.

"I just got done wrapping up some business in Orlando, I should be there in about ten minutes," he responded, sounding like he was out of breath. Before I could ask him about the gray Magnum, he hung up the phone and all I heard was the dial tone.

"Damn!" I shouted before backing out the driveway. I could see the Magnum was still parked by the time I hit the main street, but after I hit a couple side roads and punched the gas a little, I glanced at my rear view mirror, and he was right on my bumper. "Who the fuck is that?" I asked no one.

Supreme had taught me long ago how to protect myself in the worst situation, so without a second thought, I applied more pressure to the gas pedal, taking the speedometer from thirty-five to sixty miles per hour. I didn't want to do anything stupid, because I still had the drugs in the car, but at the same time, I had to do something. I drove through a shopping center, blowing my horn repeatedly, until I made it to a store that was crowded with people. I then jumped out, and screamed that I was being fol- lowed, while pointing towards the Magnum. Everybody out there just stared at me like I was crazy, and stood there like zombies.

"Don't just stand there. Call the cops," I shouted, feeling em- barrassed after hearing two teenagers snickering behind me. I turned towards them to let them have a piece of my mind and lost my train of thought once I saw the Magnum speed away out of my peripheral vision. "You know what, fuck all y'all," I shouted before running back to my car. Soon as I brought it to life and drove into oncoming traffic, my cell phone started screaming at me. "Hello?" I answered without looking at the screen.

"Where you at?"

"It's been a change of plan. Meet me at Tweety Bird," I said, soon as I realized it was Supreme. Tweety Bird was the code name I gave Supreme's second stash house because it was the only yellow house on that whole block and plus, it was really cute.

"What you mean, it's been a change of plan?" Supreme wanted to know.

"Just meet me there and I'll explain it to you later," I responded, then hung up. Ten minutes later, I was pulling in the garage of Tweety Bird while Supreme waited for me.

"You a'ight?" he asked soon as I got out of the car.

"No. I'm not a'ight!"

"What you mean?" he asked confused. I looked at him with the most senseless look I could muster, then gave him my Oscar award-winning performance.

"Somebody was fuckin' following me!" I said, with a single tear falling down my cheek. "Do you realize how scared I am right now? I know they knew I had drugs in the car, so they was gone kill me and take it."

"Hold up, baby, calm down and listen to me real good," he responded, before grabbing both sides of my face. "Who was following you, what they looked like, what color car they were in?" he asked, drilling me with questions. He was asking so many questions at one time that he had me scared to answer them, thinking I was being interrogated for something I did wrong.

"It was a gray Magnum with spinning chrome rims. It was parked in the driveway when I pulled up to the house on 23rd and 14th Street. Then when I left, it started following me. I don't know why you acting like you all concerned now, when I first tried to ask you about the Magnum, you hung up on me." He just stood there like he was deep in thought after listening to what I was saying. "Hello! Earth to Supreme," I shouted to get his attention back to me.

"I'll handle everything, bae, don't worry about it," was all he said before walking off. Soon as he took his drugs out of my car, I jumped in the driver's seat and went home. I had been driving a total of fourteen hours, so you know I was tired, and all I wanted to do was take a hot bubble bath, then go into a coma-like sleep in my bed fit for a queen.

I don't know what time it was when Supreme came crawling his ass in bed next to me, but I do know he wanted some pussy, because he did his same routine by pressing his rock-hard dick against my ass, then asking if I was awake. "I am now, thanks to you," I said with much attitude.

"C'mon, bae, I need some to put me to sleep." Now, I really wasn't in the mood to have sex at the moment, but I figured if he wanted this pussy bad enough, he would have to start from the bottom.

How bad do you need this pussy?" I asked, starting with a little foreplay.

"I need it badder then Bobby Brown need his next crack rock." I burst out laughing at him for being so silly.

"Well, you remember that song by Drake, 'Started From the Bottom'?"

"Yeah, but what that gotta do with anything?"

"That's where I want you to start, because I like my kisses down low," I responded, before pushing his face in my pussy. In no time, he had my pussy soaking wet and my clit throbbing from his skillful tongue. He literally stuck his whole tongue inside me, then flipped it to massage my G-spot.

Damn! He was driving me crazy, and I couldn't stop myself from cumming all over his face. Now, that's one thing I loved about Supreme, because before I met him, I had no idea how good head could make you feel. We call them golden heads where I'm from, somebody with that type of head that'll make a bitch wanna run up the walls and scream for Jesus! "C'mon baby, I want you to fuck me now," I moaned, pushing his head back with both hands.

"No, don't run now. This what you wanted."

"Oh yes, baby. It feels so good... Mmmmmm... don't stop." I could feel myself about to explode at any second and at that moment, tears started to blur my vision. "Oh God, fuuuuuuuuck!" I shouted as I came for the second time. Before I could jump off cloud nine from that orgasm I just had, Supreme had my knees visiting my shoulders, while sliding in me raw dog. "Shit... baby, I love you so much," I whispered in his ear once I felt his hardness brush against my sensitive clit. Supreme wasn't all that big down below, matter of fact, I'll give him a good six inches, but he damn sure knew how to use it. And that kept me satisfied.

Two minutes later, I was falling off my high horse while Supreme pulled out of me with a limp dick. Men always found a way of ruining things for a bitch after getting her hopes all up, that's why before anything ever went down between us, he gotta use his tongue to make sure I get mine. I looked at him with so much hatred, and all he could do was lay down and turn his back towards me, because he knew he had just pissed me off. I pulled most of the blanket around my body, not caring if he had any and went back to sleep, playing with my fuckin' emotions.

When I awoke the next morning, I was in my bed alone, and the sight of my naked body brought back memories of how Supreme couldn't last no more than a minute once he penetrated me. I smiled to myself before shaking my head, trying to erase that episode, because today was a new day and I actually felt kind of good. I crawled out the bed then walked to the bathroom, and that's where I stayed for the next hour, letting the shower water massage my body. Justice was an understatement to how the water did my body, because soon as I stepped out, I felt like a weight had been lifted off my shoulders.

I really didn't have any plans for the day, besides picking up Supreme's clothes from the dry cleaners, so I was debating on whether I wanted to hang out around the house or hit the Florida Mall in Orlando. I quickly made up my mind once I scanned my closet and saw my twelve-hundred-dollar Donna Karan dress with the thigh-high split Supreme bought me a couple months ago as a birthday present. I curled my hair, threw on my dress, then slid my pedicured feet into my three-and-a-half-inch stilettos before walking out the door. It was already fifteen minutes till twelve, so that meant I had about three hours to enjoy myself at the mall. Once I hopped in the car, I made it to the interstate in about ten minutes and drove I-75 all the way to Orlando, which took no more than thirty minutes, and the Florida Mall stood right in front of me.

I ran through every designer store in there at least once, so my hands were full of bags I could barely carry. I checked my cell phone to see what time it was, and it surprised me how fast it went. I couldn't believe I had been in there damn near two hours. I figured it was a good time to call it a day and started towards the exit, when my stomach started growling at me. I knew I hadn't eaten all day. And the sweet aroma of their foreign food had me ready to force the Chinese restaurant out of business from eating all their damn food. I turned towards the food court, and walked over there to place my order, and the craziest thing happened. None of them muthafuckas spoke a lick of English, so you know I was pissed off.

"Excuse me, can you go get somebody who speaks English? Because I don't understand a word you're saying, and I'm ready to order my food," I said to the Chinese lady standing at the cash register. I wasn't sure, but I think she caught an attitude, because the tone of her voice rose, and she started rolling her neck like she had a crook in it. I burst into laughter not being able to hold it any longer, and spit flew everywhere. I tried to apologize, but I couldn't control myself and at that point, my whole facial expression changed once I saw Ms. Bruce Lee jump over the counter, and sprint towards me with a butcher's knife. I felt like a deer caught in headlights as I just stood there contemplating my next move. I knew I had to think of something real fast, but what? So, I did what anybody would do in a situation such as this and got the hell up out of there, almost breaking my heel in the process.

I made it to my car in three minutes flat, with my arms still full of bags and breathing like a sumo wrestler. "Damn, that bitch was trying to stab me," I said, almost out of breath. I checked my handbag for my .45, then found my way back towards the entrance of the mall after throwing my shopping bags into the car.

"Excuse me, ma'am, are you alright?" I heard a voice ask, stopping me in my tracks. I tried to turn around, but my whole body felt frozen as my heart started beating like four fifteen-inch subwoofers in my chest. "Ma'am!" he said again once I didn't respond. When I finally turned to face him, I quickly released my gun, and snatched my hand out of my bag, because he was the last person I wanted to see at the moment. "Ma'am, I'm Officer Brown, and I just saw everything that happened. Are you alright?" he asked, then continued before I could answer. "Please rest assured that I'm not going to let her stay out here and continue to harass the Florida Mall shoppers."

I really wasn't a police person, so he was just wasting his time. *I'm a grown ass woman and I could take care of my own problems*, I thought as I told him I was alright and headed back to my car, because I knew my chance of getting that bitch back was now slim to none. Once I got inside my car, I burned rubber leaving out of the parking lot, only to be
sideswiped by a black Lexis coupe that looked exactly like the one Supreme drives. The worse part about it was that the muthafucka kept going. I was stunned, because the little tap almost caused me to lose control of my car at the speed I was going.

Once I gained my composure and ignored all the people blowing their horns because I was holding up traffic, I stepped on the gas, and grabbed my cell phone out of my bag. "Baby, where are you?" I asked once Supreme answered his phone.

"I'm at Tweety Bird taking care of business, why?" he responded. Now I was really getting pissed off, because he just told me a bold face lie, and he knew lying was one thing we didn't do to each other. I knew that was him, because the tag on the car had the initials S.O.D., which stood for Supreme On Deck. "I just wanted to know. Call me when you're on your way home. Love you," I said, playing the role of the dumb bitch he thought I was before hanging up.

By this time, I was about four or five cars behind him, taking every left and right turn he made, determined to find out the reason he lied to me. Fifteen minutes later, he was driving into an upscale neighborhood with luxury cars and white picket fences, and he still hadn't realized he was being followed. I tapped my brake pedal every couple seconds to ease further behind the three cars in front of me, and to see what Supreme's next move would be. He pulled up to a two-story brick house that could easily be mistaken as a mini mansion, with three beautiful automobiles parked in the circular driveway. I was amazed by this castle, which was fitted for a royal family, but what really caught my attention was one of the three automobiles. A gray Magnum with twenty-six-inch spinning chrome rims. I knew I had seen it before, but I couldn't figure out where exactly. I sat in my car parked across the street and thought for twenty minutes, until it hit me. This was the same car that followed me when I came back from Atlanta with the drugs. The same car I was telling Supreme about, before he told me he would take care of it.

I took a deep breath and wiped my face with both hands. I needed to figure out what was really going on, because this shit was getting crazier by the second. Supreme had been in the house for about twenty or twenty-five minutes now, which I figured was plenty of time for him to make a transaction, if that was the type of business he was talking about taking care of. I reached inside my purse, grabbed my .45 and checked the magazine, making sure it was fully loaded, before stepping out of my car like the gangsta bitch I was. My adrenaline was pumpin' from being so anxious to find out what was going on inside that beautiful house, but at the same time, the silence of the atmosphere was turning me into a nervous wreck. There were no dogs barking, or the sound of traffic, and that made me feel like somebody was watching me. I crept up to the side of the house, then looked in every direction before focusing inside the window like a peeping Tom. The sun had started to set, and all the lights on the lower part of the house were turned off, so I couldn't see a damn thing. "Shit!" I cursed the sun for taking away my light at the time I needed it the most. Once I realized that part of my plan was a dead deal, I proceeded back towards the front door like I was a visitor. Well, a welcome visitor.

I wanted so badly to find out what was going on, and why I let myself get caught up in trusting men again, when I told myself it would never happen. The closer I came to reaching the front door, the more nervous I was. My palms were starting to get sweaty and I kind of felt like I was running a fever from how hot and queasy my body became. "Mahogany, girl, you can do this," I said to myself, while clutching the doorknob with my left hand and my .45 with my right.

Once I turned it then gave a light push the door opened like magic, and I proceeded on my mission. I had to adjust my eyes to the darkness once I entered, but I was soon convinced that this part of the house was empty as I made my way to the staircase. Two at a time, I took the stairs until I made it all the way up to the second level of the house. I could hear voices coming from the back, but they sounded like they were being muffled or either moans of pain. The closer I got, the louder it became until I was standing right outside the door it was coming from. I could see pictures of all kind of crazy shit going on in my head as I imagined what was happening on the other side of this door. I took a deep breath preparing myself for what I might see, then counted to three before turning the knob and pushing the door open.

"What the fuck!" I yelled, not believing my eyes as they started to water. All the preparing in the world couldn't get me ready for what I was seeing. Supreme jumped to his feet and just stared at me, knowing the look in my eyes all too well. I guess he never saw the gun I had in my hand, because soon as I raised it to aim at his head, his eyes became full of terror. "After everything I've done for you, this is how you repay me?" I said, eyes full of tears. "My daddy always told me being disloyal won't get you nowhere, but six feet deep on some white man's property," I finished, and then applied
pressure to my trigger before closing my eyes, as the gun jumped around in my hand.

## Chapter Two
### E'mani

"Some people want it all...but I don't want nothing at all...If it ain't you, baby, if I ain't got you, baby," I sang along with Alicia Keys as I stared at my naked body in my wall-length mirror. Five foot two, light-colored skin and a big round phat booty, I was fine and far from a dime. My mother is Filipino, and my father is from Jamaica so yes, I am very unique. I had long curly hair down my back until I recently got it cut like the singer Toni Braxton. Now people say I remind them of the actress Halle Berry.

I just got home from class at the University of Central Florida, where I'm studying to get my master's degree in accounting. That's where I met Supreme two years ago. My boyfriend had just dumped me after I told him I missed my period and I thought I was pregnant. I couldn't stop the tears from coming down my face, because I loved him with everything in me. And to make the situation worse, he was the one I gave my virginity to. He left me standing in the front of his dorm as he walked off with his friends like I never mattered to him. I thought my life was over without him, and at that very moment I had thoughts of committing suicide. I walked back to my dorm and daydreamed about me dying if I got hit by a car, while I continued to cry. I was so deep in my thoughts that I never realized how close I was to incoming traffic, until my feet slipped off the side of the curb, and I went tumbling in front of an F-150 truck with huge chrome rims. To make a long story short, the truck stopped inches from my body, and out jumped Supreme with the swagger of a man who was sitting on millions of dollars. From there it seemed like we just clicked, because one thing led to another and now, I'm his girl and his accountant. I knew that Supreme was a drug dealer, but I wanted and needed a little excitement in my life, so I took a chance. Once I threw on my PJ's, I jumped in bed and grabbed the remote control to surf the channels, looking for my favorite show *Love & Hip Hop*, so I could relax. I was quickly disappointed as I found out the show had just gone off. Missing my show had really taken a lot excitement out of my mood, so I grabbed the papers off my nightstand, and went over all Supreme's financial records.

Yes, I had access to all of his accounts, savings account, checking account, business account, and even his safe deposit box. I handled every penny he owned and could get to it whenever I wanted, so it surprised me when I saw he withdrew two hundred thousand dollars from his business account, and twenty thousand from his checking account two days ago, without notifying me. I made a mental note to ask him about it the next day, then pulled out my diary of poems to record the poem of the day, before calling it a night.

*Friday, June 29, 2018*
*9:30 p.m.*

*"My Feelings For You"*

*How I feel about you is too hard to explain. Something like explaining to a child how babies are really made. I can't just say I love you, that's too simple of a word. I want you to get high off of what I say. I'm talking higher than a bird. My feelings for you. I'm talking precious diamonds after going through its stages of roughness to shininess. I can keep fumbling with words all night until I find the right one, like I found you or should I say like you found me, but this where it ends, not permanently only temporary, so while I'm sleeping, I'm going to keep trying to find the words to explain to you, or should I say my feelings for you.*

V Mani V

Saturday, I woke up feeling like I had a hangover as I drug myself out of bed to hit the snooze button on my screaming alarm clock. I really wasn't in the mood to do anything today. I swear, all I wanted to do was pull my comforter back over my head, and be dead to the world for a couple more hours. But I decided otherwise and crawled out the bed to go empty my bladder.

Once I was done relieving myself, I washed my hands then stepped on the scale to weigh myself. I just started Weight Watchers a couple weeks ago and have to confess to sticking my hands in the cookie jar once or twice, maybe even three times. One forty-five, it read. Ten minutes later, I was still looking down at the scale, hoping the numbers would change. I was disappointed with myself, because while I was supposed to be losing weight, I had gained five more pounds in the last couple weeks. I stepped off the scale and ran me some bath water before returning to my bedroom. I couldn't enjoy my shower without my strawberry-scented body wash, which I bought from Bath and Body Works, so that was the first thing I grabbed. Back in the bathroom, I undressed myself, then eased my way into the steaming hot water as it ran. It didn't take long at all to get used to once I lathered my rag with body wash and washed my entire body.

The last fifteen minutes, I laid my head back on the end of the tub and enjoyed the silence. The water started to get cold after about ten minutes, so I decided to get out and dry off. My skin was feeling so soft and smooth, I was tempted to stand there and rub myself until I got tired, but that thought quickly vanished once I felt the cold air brush across my naked body. I rushed to my room where it was a little more comfortable, being that I kept my thermostat at a fair temperature and caught a glimpse of myself in the mirror. I was twenty-five years old, in college, and didn't have any kids running around everywhere. Tell me I wasn't a man's idea of a real woman. I stared in the mirror for about ten whole minutes, like I had caught myself doing on the regular the last couple weeks. I just couldn't stop looking at my tummy. It was so flat. I wanted abs, but I hated working out, so I don't know how that was gone happen.

After a while, I threw on a pair of blue denim jeans and a white blouse, which complemented my figure, then curled my hair to bring out the unique features of my foreign background. Once I was done getting dressed, I threw on a pair of sunglasses to shield my vision from any future haters I might run into while I was out. "You the one that I think about all da-a-ay." My cellphone rang and caught my attention as Rihanna sang about the special person in her life at the time. A smile forced its way onto my face, because without looking at the screen, I already knew who was calling. "Hey, baby!" I answered excitedly. When I didn't get a reply, I repeated myself. "Hey, baby." Still no answer. "Hel-loooo... Supreme, baby!" I yelled until I got tired. I took the phone away from my ear for a minute to see if he had hung up on me, but he hadn't. The lines were still connected. Once I brought it back I could hear talking, but it sounded like it was at a distance. I blocked everything out and listened a little closer.

"Wait! Supreme, where are you going?" I heard a female ask. Now I was mad, but I guess Supreme ignored her, because I could hear him telling somebody else to get rid of her, and meet him at his spot on 23rd and 14th. When I heard another female reply in a flirtatious manner that she'll handle it, I wanted to scream and throw my phone against the wall, but I knew that would be stupid of me, because I'm the one who would have to replace it.

Soon as I hung up the phone, I was out the house and headed to my car. I had three but for this mission I had to be mindful of which one I chose, so I hopped in my Dodge, which was the only car of mine that had tinted windows, so I wouldn't be seen so easily. I slowly pulled out of my circular driveway and blended in with traffic, on my way to I-75. From Orlando to Deland was only about thirty minutes, give or take, so I just cruised to give myself time to think. The thirty-minute drive took about forty-five, and the house was deserted when I got there. I reached inside my purse and grabbed my cell to dial Supreme's number, just to locate his destination.

Out of nowhere, a white Honda Accord pulled up in the driveway, which scared the hell out of me, causing me to drop my phone. Now, I knew the driver couldn't see me through the tinted windows, but that didn't stop her from trying. Yes, I said her. I knew for sure that it was a female, because I was staring the heifer right in her face. I picked my phone up off the floor, but wouldn't let myself take my eyes off her. I was like a lion stalking her prey.

After about five minutes, she pulled out her phone, and made a call. I couldn't read her lips, but I could tell she was going off on the person who was on the receiving end, because her body language was that of a woman who was pissed off. All of a sudden, she hit her steering wheel with a closed fist before backing out of the driveway. I waited until her car disappeared on the next street before I started to follow. My mind was racing with so many thoughts, and I had to find out who this woman was, because I wasn't letting her take my man. Not even five minutes had passed before I knew I was caught. She was starting to pick up speed in an attempt to elude me, so I knew even by being three cars behind her, I was still visible to her eyes.

I continued my chase as she led me to an overcrowded shopping center while repeatedly blowing her horn as she drove. I was confused, because I didn't know what kind of game she was playing. Why would she do that? I soon found out once she jumped out of her car and pointed towards me causing everybody around her to look my way. She was screaming at the top of her lungs, stealing the attention of the shopping center customers. Once more, people started gathering around, and disregarding the reason they were there in the first place. I knew it was time for me to leave. I burned the rubber off my new tires trying to get away from there, not caring that I had just spent a hundred dollars a piece on four brand-new tires seven days ago. I drove all the way back to Orlando, feeling like detective scary cat because I didn't even get to find out who she was or what she was doing at my man's place. I guess I'll just have to charge it to the game and hope next time I have luck on my side.

When I got back to my city, I drove around for almost an hour, watching the sun set and enjoying the light breeze the night brought. I was still a little pissed off from hearing Supreme tell that woman to meet him at his place, but a lot of time had passed, and I figured if it was meant for me to know who she was, I'll find out. I made the familiar drive back to my domain, and circled my driveway parking directly in front of my house. The first thing I did upon entering the house was run straight to the shower. I didn't even grab my nightclothes or panties before I was naked.

Before I knew it, fifteen minutes had turned into thirty, and thirty into sixty. The water just felt so good as I stood there while it caressed my body. I closed my eyes and tilted my head back to feel more pressure on my sensitive areas, and it was like my hands had their own mind as they traveled down my body to squeeze my nipples and fondle my sleek clitoris. "Ahhh..." I moaned, before biting down on my bottom lip and easing one, then two fingers into my wet kitty. I was so wet my fingers slid in without resistance, and my body exploded with pleasure as my knees became weak, and my legs started to buckle. The hard texture of a rough hand brushed across my midsection, causing me to jump, and open my eyes in fear.

"Having fun?" a male voice asked.

I smiled at the familiar face. It was very erotic the way he stood naked, with his gorgeous tool resting in the palm of his hand. He stepped closer and began whispering what he would like to do to me. He started rubbing my breasts, and kissing my neck, while at the same time murmuring about all the sensual things he wanted to do to me, like how he wanted to stick his tongue up my kitty, rub his face all around my hot wet crotch, and suck my clit 'til I cum! I was so horny from his words that I took his hand and placed it between my legs so he could feel how wet he made me. His fingers came alive as he started fingering me.

"Damn, baby, let's take this to the bed," I moaned while gasping for air. Without warning, I got out of the tub, dried myself and went into my bedroom while he followed. He gently laid me down on my bed, and began to stroke the inside of my thighs, opening my legs to lick and lap at my wet kitty, sending me into spasms of desire and wanting desperately to be sexed. My baby was licking along the inside of my labia, still not putting his tongue inside me fully. I moaned to him about how hot he was making me, and how I could feel an orgasm coming on. I told him to finish me off by sexing me with that golden head, and without warning, he removed his tongue and replaced it with his huge dick.

"Ahhhh..." I gasped for air as he went deep enough to the point where I felt him in my chest. "What the hell is wrong with you?" I asked after catching my breath and slapping him across the face. He stared in my eyes and smiled, continuing his in and out motion, causing my kitty to feel so much pleasure. "Mmm. Baby, I love you," I whispered as a single tear dropped from my eye.

He sexed me to my final orgasm, or should I say his final orgasm, because it wasn't over until he came deep inside me. We laid in bed for about ten minutes, catching our breath, before I sat upon my elbows and looked him directly in the face. "I saw your little girlfriend in Deland," I stated. "She lucky I didn't get out my car and get ghetto, because if she would've did anything other than drive off and run from me, that's exactly what I would've did."

Laying on his back with both eyes closed, he replied, "That ain't my girlfriend. She was a business partner. That's why she was at my stash house. And for the record, don't you ever pull that shit again like you pulled today."

I just rolled my eyes and changed the subject, because I knew I stepped out of my boundary when I went to Deland looking for trouble. "Two hundred and twenty thousand dollars had been withdrawn from your business checking account three days ago. Would you mind telling me why you didn't notify me?" I asked.

His eyes were still closed as he responded. "That was my fault, baby, but I didn't want to cause any suspicion by you withdrawing that amount of money, so I just did it myself. I'm sorry I didn't inform you."

That was all the conversation I got out of him before his cellphone rang and he told me he had to make a run but promised to call me in the morning. I let him leave without protesting, because I was kind of exhausted anyway. I then grabbed my poem book before calling it a night.

*Saturday, June 30, 2018*

*11:38 pm.*
*"How do you do it"*

*You've only been gone five minutes, but yet I miss you like it's been a decade. I could still feel the pressure of your body on top of mine, our lips dancing with each other, and your manhood tickling my kitty... Damn! You make me scream words that I never even knew was in my vocabulary. How do you do it? How do you make me want you with so much desire that it feels like my whole body's on fire, or how you minimize the pain, and make me come like falling rain? Please tell me, because I'm dying to know how do you do it.*

*Signed, Mani*

The next morning, I woke up with Supreme on my mind. I'm pretty sure it had everything to do with him being the last thing on my mind before I went to sleep last night, or me dreaming about him. Whichever one it was, I had to grab my poem book to write this entry that had me feeling sticky.

*Sunday, July 1, 2018*
*10:45 a.m.*
*"Da Dream"*

*If every woman in the world had her own miracle worker, then you'll be mine. Mr. Kitty Kat Pleaser is what I'll call you, because nothing can compare to the way you tease me then eat me with the skills of an animal. You have me wondering sometimes if you were taught by a woman, because a man is just not capable of learning that on his own. Mr. Kitty Kat Pleaser, I whispered three times as I lay in my bed with my eyes closed and legs spread wide, while you go to work doing miracles on my kitty. But then I awake alone with my hands deep in my jammies, Da' Dream seems so real, but now I have to change my panties.*

*Signed, Mani*

I smiled after closing my book, because just writing that poem had me feeling moist between my legs. I ignored the feeling though, because today was Sunday and Pastor Tolver was expecting me to lead the choir after his sermon at 11:3O, so that meant I needed to get ready. I took a quick shower before searching my closet for a dress to wear. Once I found one with the heels to match, I did my make-up, checked myself in the mirror one more time, then grabbed my purse and continued to my car.

It didn't take long before I was parked right outside Grace Bible Church of Central Florida, on Dorscher Road. I looked around and there were cars everywhere, so that meant I was late. I figure Pastor Tolver would understand, being that I lived all the way on the other side of town. My mother's gray Oldsmobile was parked in front of the church as it has been every Sunday for the last fourteen years, so I knew I had better get my butt in there, or I would be hearing her mouth about being late for my weekly meeting with God on his special day.

I crept through the door, trying to go unseen by the congregation to take my position before the choir sang their first song.

"Loyalty," I heard Pastor Tolver shout. "All God wants from you is loyalty. I don't know about your God, but my God is a jealous God."

"Amen, Pastor!" a woman stood up and shouted.

At that instant the door let off a loud squeak, compliments of the rusted-out hinges. The whole congregation turned my way as I stood there caught, and embarrassed. All eyes were on me as I carefully walked down the aisle, hugged Pastor Tolver, then stood in front of the choir.

"You provide the fire, I'll provide the sacrifice. You pour out your spirit, I will open up inside. Fill me up, God." I started singing the song "Fill Me Up" by Tasha Cobbs to play off the embarrassment I felt and to my surprise, the whole choir joined in at the perfect time, making the ordeal seem planned.

"Amen, baby. Sang it for Him. Give Him all the glory." Sister Odelle shouted as she stoodup with both her hands in the air. It was like a domino effect once Sister Green stood up, followed by Sister Williams, Sister Davis, Sister Brown, and Sister Smith. The next time I looked up, the whole congregation was on their feet, while some took the initiative to even sing along. "Fill meeee uppp, God. Fill meeee uppp, God. Fill meeee uppp, God."

Everybody gave a round of applause as I finished, while my mother winked at me to let me know she was proud. I felt like a celebrity once I saw the line of people with their hands out to greet me as I walked to sit next to my mother.

"Baby, you did a good job up there today," my mother said and hugged me. We sat through two hours of Pastor Tolver's sermon about love, loyalty, and how even the little things we do can affect the way we're viewed in life. It really touched me, and made me think about my life, and where it was headed. Life was too short to have regrets or hold grudges, so if you were blessed to still have loved ones to support you, you have to hold on to them.

Around 2:30 p.m., people started making their way towards the front door and to their cars. I told Mama to drive safe, and that I would call her soon as I made it home myself. I hopped in my car and drove, with a million thoughts on my mind. Mostly how I was blessed to have all the advantages I had throughout my life, and never really had to go through the struggle as people say.

I arrived home in no time, and cooked myself something to eat before undressing, wearing only boy short panties, and a bra. I felt more comfortable this way as I ate, and relaxed almost dozing off as I watched TV.

"Baby, where are you?" I heard a male voice ask. I jumped up off the bed feeling so excited, because I knew it had to be Supreme. He was the only other person besides me that had a key to my house.

"I'm upstairs in my room," I replied. Not even two minutes later, I saw Supreme standing in my doorway, staring at me like I looked good enough to eat. I waited until I was just inches away, before jumping into his arms and showering his face with kisses. He responded quickly by removing my panties and bra, and I laid naked in his arms. He, too, shed all his clothes to be nude as I was as our bodies threshed wildly towards my bed. He laid me down and opened my legs to expose my already dampening kitty. His head shot straight between them, and I clamped my thighs around it as his mouth glued itself to my kitty. His trembling fingers parted my lips, and he licked it from bottom to top. I writhed with ecstasy as his fingers now penetrated my soaked womanhood, and he sucked the engorged clit between his full lips. He mashed it hard as his fingers darted in and out, to be followed by the most lascivious licking, and lapping of his skillful tongue. I soon felt myself about to cum, and I scrunched my thighs tightly against his head as he teased out my oozing juices, lapping up my cum, savoring its salty taste. I shut my eyes tightly, enjoying the waves of pleasure traveling through my entire body, then arched my back once his tongue found my clit again.

"What the fuck!" I heard a female yell, causing my eyes to fly open in terror. Supreme jumped to his feet from between my legs, his face glistening with my cum. I scooted back until I was stopped by my headboard, covers wrapped around my naked body and in the fetal position. I was terrified of this woman with the gun in her hand. She raised it, aiming directly at Supreme's head, and I would never forget the terror I saw in his eyes.

"Baby, it's not what it look like. Think about what you're doing, you're upset right now. Don't make a permanent decision, because of a temporary emotion," he pleaded.

"After everything I've done for you, this is how you repay me?" she said, her eyes full of tears. "My daddy always told me being disloyal won't get you nowhere but six feet deep on some white man's property." She started firing.

I was so scared, I sat frozen with my eyes closed tight. I screamed at the top of my lungs, while the shots rang out rapidly and continued screaming until I heard the gun click. When I finally opened my eyes, there were bullet holes everywhere. My bedroom window was shattered. That had to be where Supreme jumped out, I concluded, since he was nowhere to be found. He had literally gotten ghost, as they say.

Keith Williams

## Chapter Three
### E'mani

I stood in my bedroom pissed off as this white officer interrogated me like I was the one who did something wrong. I was told they were called by my neighbor, saying she heard notable gunshots coming from my house, before seeing a naked man jumping out of my room window. I was so ready for them to get out, that I made up a story about meeting a man named John. I told them we met at the Florida Mall a couple hours ago and from there, we came back to my place for a nightcap. I knew I was making myself look like a whore, but I didn't care at that moment. I continued to explain that once we made it to my house, we engaged in sexual intercourse for about thirty minutes, until we were interrupted by a woman brandishing a handgun and then she started shooting. They asked me to give a description and I explained that all I saw was a slim figure with dark skin before I hid, and closed my eyes. I also told them she was screaming at him, asking how could he cheat on her, then when the shooting stopped, I opened my eyes and John was jumping out of the window, while she was on her way out the room and headed to the front door.

After a while, they started towards the door to leave, considering their work here was done for the time being, but I'm sure they saw the disgusted look on my face after I overheard the white officer tell his partner that he knew I was lying to them. I walked them to the door making sure they didn't take anything that didn't belong to them. Even though my mother was a Christian woman, she always taught me to hate cops, because they were the ones getting away with killing our people.

Once they were gone, I walked into my kitchen to get myself a stiff drink. I wasn't at all a drinker, but after everything I had went through today, I had to get me a bottle. I wanted something strong and I always heard brown liquor was the strongest, so I got a bottle of VSOP, and overlooked the white. I poured a glass and slowly sipped it, enjoying the burning sensation down my throat. Soon my whole body became numb, and I felt like I didn't have any worries as I stood to my feet. As I took a step, it was like my feet fell from under me and I went down hard. I stayed on the floor for a while, because my whole kitchen was in front of me, and I felt like I was about to start vomiting everywhere. For a minute, I was wondering what was going on, until it hit me. I was drunk for the first time, was all I thought as I laid flat on the cold floor.

The next morning, I was awakened by my screaming cell-phone. My head felt like it had been slammed in between a car door, and my body reeked with alcohol. I struggled to get up off the floor in order to make sense of what happened last night, but I don't think my brain was functioning properly, because I couldn't. I knew I was already late for class today, and walking into my room seeing one thirty p.m. on my alarm clock confirmed it. That meant today I was playing hooky. My cell phone rang once again reminding me why I came up to my room. I picked it up, and tapped the screen before putting it to my ear.

"E'mani Shanel Newman!" my mother shouted. "What the hell is going on? Are you alright? They have your house all over the news, talking about somebody was shooting. Now you tell me something right now, because you know I did not raise you to be a hoodlum."

I wanted to hang up so bad, because I was definitely not in the mood, but I knew if I did that I wouldn't hear the end of it. "Ma, I'm alright. It was just a really big misunderstanding. Don't believe everything they say on the news, and for the shooting, that was my neighbor and her husband," I replied. I felt so bad lying to my mother, and I knew God was not going to let me into the gates of heaven if I kept this up. But I did it for her own good. I didn't want to stress her out by worrying about me. She was already old. After I calmed my mother's nerves and convinced her I was in fact, not hurt, I hung up the phone and called a handyman to patch up the bullet holes in my walls and replace the shattered window, before jumping in the shower.

Ten minutes turned into twenty, and twenty into thirty, like always. I couldn't help it. I get in the shower sometimes and get lost. Once I got out, I dried myself, then walked into my room, feeling sexy and free as the sun peeped through my window and licked my naked body. *Today felt like it was going to be a good day, despite what took place yesterday*, I thought as I glided to my dresser while dragging my feet on the feather soft carpet. Before I could find me a pair of panties my cellphone rang forcing me to change the direction I was going. "Hello!" I answered in an aggravated tone, not recognizing the number. I waited for the person to respond and God is my witness, I would have never thought in a million years, I would be talking to the person I was talking to at this moment.

Keith Williams

### Chapter Four
**Mahogany**

I drove straight to the interstate and rode I-75 all the way back to Deland, doing close to eighty miles per hour. My mind was stuck on this other woman. I wasn't psychic or anything, but I was willing to bet the roundness of my phat ass that she was probably thinking I was chasing after Supreme. But if she knew like I knew, I didn't give a fuck about him at that moment. I was trying to get the hell from out of there before the police showed up. My gun sat on the passenger seat, my adrenaline was pumpin' a million miles per hour, and I felt like I was out of control. I guess all the times I was telling myself that I wished Supreme would cheat on me, thinking I was a boss bitch finally came back to bite me in the ass.

That's why old people are always saying be careful what you wish for, because you just might get it. I could still feel my wrist jerking as I drove with both hands on the steering wheel. I had never been in a situation where I had to actually fire my gun, but I now see why people carry theirs everywhere they go and are quick to pull it out to shoot somebody. The power you feel when you know everybody is running and hiding because of you is really addictive.

Supreme's car wasn't parked in the driveway when I made it home, so that meant I had enough time to change the locks and throw all his shit out before he showed up. I had a feeling he was probably thinking all he had to do was lay low for a couple days and then come home, and everything would be alright, like he did the last time we had an argument about him bringing dope where we laid our heads at.

This was different though. He fucked up bad this time and I was tired of his shit. Once the locksmith finished and he was paid, I went to our closet, the side Supreme kept his clothes on and just stood there at first, looking at all the nice things he owned. I mean, he had a lot of expensive shit and some even still had tags on them. Everything inside of me wanted to grab all his shit, soak it with bleach, then set a match to it and watch the colors of the flames. But I couldn't do it, because that would be some flaw shit, and everybody knew Mahogany wasn't a flaw ass bitch. I was stuck standing there not knowing what I should do.

"I was so fuckin' loyal to you, stupid ass muthafucka, and all you had to do was the same in return, but no, you had to be thinking with your dick," I screamed, pouring out all the anger I had built up inside of me as I dropped down to my hands and knees crying like a baby. Supreme and I had been together for eight years, and my love for him had always been deeper than the Atlantic Ocean, but I could now feel it all fading away like he never mattered. I've always been a loyal ass bitch and when I love someone, I love with everything inside of me, but when I'm betrayed, I also hate with every inch of my soul, and won't stop until revenge is served cold. Time was ticking and I could literally feel myself transitioning into a whole new person as I let my anger take control of my body like I was possessed. Everything I've ever been through in my life started flashing before my eyes, and I could feel the blood as I squeezed my fist so tight that my nails started cutting into the palm of my hands. Memories of how kids used to pick on me in school, and call me Cat Woman Black, because I had dark skin with green eyes. And how my own cousin held me down and raped me when I was only twelve years old, taking my innocence. So many memories came rushing back at once that it felt like my head was going to explode, and I couldn't do anything to stop it if I wanted to. I screamed at the top of my lungs over and over again, trying to make them go away, but they wouldn't. My whole body became overheated as my blood boiled like hot lava, and within a split second, I felt my body go limp and my eyes being forced closed as I blacked out.

Twelve hours later, I was awakened by the rising of the sun peeking through my window, forcing my eyelids open. Supreme still hadn't come home, but it didn't matter anymore, because his actions now showed me where we stood in this relationship. He didn't give a damn about me, and it felt good to finally say our feelings were mutual. I walked into the master bathroom to splash a little cold water on my face, and to clean myself up, because I was a hot mess. My hair was matted on my head, and my makeup was so smeared it resembled mud on my skin. I washed my face, then looked at my reflection in the mirror, and my eyes were the one thing that caught my attention. They were so dark that whoever stared into them would be able to see the story of my past. The pain I endured and the hatred I felt for so many people.

After a little while, I was led back to my room where I stumbled upon a white business card that seemed to have appeared out of nowhere. The card read, E'mani Newman with an Orlando, Florida address and phone number at the bottom. Things like this usually didn't catch my interest, but the fact that it had the city of Orlando on it made me really curious. Curious enough to call it.

"May I speak to E'mani?" I asked as soon as she greeted me with a hello.

"It's pronounced E'moni, but this is she." Right then, I knew this was the same woman I had caught Supreme with. Her voice sounded too familiar and from the way she was screaming yesterday, I don't think I'll ever forget it.

"I know I'm the last person you probably want to hear from right now, but—"

"Who is this? Do I know you?" she interrupted, then asked.

"You do, but you don't," I started. "I'm the woman that showed up to your house yesterday, shooting like a maniac."

"OmiGod!" she shouted.

"Please don't hang up. I just want to talk to you."

"You tried to kill me yesterday."

"Well, actually I tried to kill Supreme, but I wanted to know if we could get together and talk about yesterday?" I asked in a hesitant manner. She agreed after I convinced her that I wasn't going to finish what I started yesterday once I got to her house.

It took me close to an hour to get myself together once I ended my phone call. Between taking a shower and flat ironing my hair, I was about thirty minutes away from being late for my meeting with E'mani. We both agreed to act like young ladies, but I didn't really know her like that so if she wanted to get on some gangsta shit when I got there, I was on that. I reloaded the magazine to my

.45 and tossed it into my handbag before walking to my car. I just felt like a whole new person as the wind tackled me, almost causing me to have a Marilyn Monroe moment. I smiled to myself, because I had always wondered what she was thinking about when that happened, and now I knew. She was trying to keep the world from looking at her goodies, because she didn't have on panties. At least that's what I was thinking at the moment.

I pulled up in front of E'mani's house in no time. Florida's traffic wasn't all that bad especially after happy hour, so I wasn't late getting there. Her house still surprised me from how big it was, but it also brought back memories. I took one big deep breath, then got out the car, and proceeded to knock on the door. She answered after about a minute, then invited me in to take a seat on the couch. Once she took a seat right across from me, we just stared at each other not saying a word until the silence got the best of me.

"How did you meet Supreme, and how long have you two been having this fling?"

"Fling?" she said with attitude. "We didn't have a fling. He's my man. We've been together two and a half years now."

"Two and a half years?" I shouted, cutting her off.

"Yes, two and a half years," she replied with a smile. At that moment, my head began to throb. I couldn't believe Supreme was cheating on me for two and a half years, and I never saw it. How fuckin' blind and stupid could I be? She continued to brag about how Supreme bought her this house after only being with her for two years at the time. And how he helped pay her way through college to get her bachelor's degree in business. Now she's working on getting her masters in accounting. She told me that she was also his accountant, and had access to every last one of his accounts, so their relationship had to be more than a fling.

I couldn't lie. I felt some type of way after hearing all this, but I knew Supreme and I were over for good, and there was no chance of us getting back together, so I had to control my feelings. We both sat there quiet, and stared at each other again. I was thinking about my next move because I really wanted to pull my gun out, and use this bitch as target practice, but I didn't. I also promised her it wasn't going to be a part two of what happened about twenty-four hours ago.

I smiled to myself as she gave me her wicked stare. I guess she was trying to intimidate me, but my mind was turning this whole situation around on Supreme's ass, and making him regret ever being disloyal. I needed her help on pulling this off though, and I knew just the way to get her. Make her feel guilty.

"For eight long years, I made that man the center of my universe. I've had two miscarriages in three years, put my life on the line once a week, and I would've put a bullet in any bitch's head if he would've asked me to," I said, making my eyes water. I didn't know if she was buying it, but I was gone keep going until I knew. "He used to tell me he loved me, and how beautiful I was so much that I didn't believe him until he got on one knee and asked me to marry him." Once I saw her wipe the tears from her eyes, then look up at me with the most regretful look I saw since I got there, I knew I had her. But then she asked the question that made me think she had caught on to my game.

"If he loved you so much, why he consistently made love to me?"

"Because he's a dog and that's what dogs do, fuck every woman they can, and tell her he loves her while doing so," I shot back recovering quickly from the bluntness of her question. She sat quietly, staring off in space like she was deep in thought, and then she frowned. "That bastard!" she shouted. I knew I had her then and to keep myself from showing my excitement, I had to bow my head, and put my hands over my mouth to keep a smile from appearing.

"You're the same girl I followed that day in the white Honda Accord?" she asked.

"Yep, that's me," I replied.

"I asked Supreme about you that same day, after he made love to me, and he said you was only a business partner. How can I be so stupid? He's just like the rest of the men out there. I should've listened to my mother when she told me to leave him." I looked at her and shook my head like I felt sorry, but deep down inside I was laughing my ass off, because she fell for the okey-doke, and my plan was coming together. After I explained to her how I wanted to make Supreme pay, and she agreed to help me, I told her the next move she should take, and got up to leave, but not before giving her my cell number.

I drove all the way to Atlanta, only stopping for gas once I left Orlando. My next move was to get Doe Boy on my side, and being that he never liked Supreme, it wouldn't be hard. I pulled up to Magic City and as always, it was deserted, so I proceeded to the front door. After about a minute I was let in, and greeted by Doe Boy.

"Nice to see you again Ms. Mahogany, but I know it ain't that time of the week already?" he asked in a confused manner. I was so nervous that I could literally feel my heart about to beat out of my chest, but I was too far gone so I knew I had to get myself together and handle my business. "No, that's not what I'm here for." I paused, before looking around for eavesdroppers. "Can we go somewhere with a little more privacy?" I asked. Without saying another word, Doe Boy led the way to his office and locked the door once we entered. I felt even more nervous now, but before I could let it get the best of me, I dropped down to my knees, and had Doe Boy's dick out of his jeans and in my mouth soon as he turned to face me.

"Oh shit!" he whispered in shock to cover the moans that almost slipped out, once my hot wet tongue lapped across the head of his shaft. I forced his back against the door and opened my mouth wider as I got into my groove, deep throating the whole length of his dick. He wasn't all that big, but he definitely wasn't small like the rumors portrayed him to be, so I was really putting in work. He then grabbed the back of my head and guided himself in and out of my mouth, while I massaged his sensitive sack and tried to swallow every last inch of his swollen dick. Damn, he tasted so good. I wasn't planning on fucking him, but I was getting so wet from sucking his dick, my pussy was dripping like a faucet. He moaned that he was about to cum and I withdrew my mouth, then squeezed the base of his dick to stop the flow, a trick I learned from watching Cherokee do her thing. I then slipped out of my jeans and laid flat across his desk on my stomach, before spreading my cheeks so he had a closer view of my pink pussy.

"Damn, it's amazing the way it's winking at me," he stated, watching as I squeezed my inner walls together, then quickly released them. I pushed my ass out towards him, hoping he got the hint that I was ready to feel something hard inside me. He responded by rubbing his dick from the top of my pussy to the crack of my ass, and then he entered me so slow that I was actually ready to beg him for it. With every in and out motion, he took my breath away with his mouth, sucking me, tonguing me, and kissing me with so much passion, I felt like I was about to explode and cum everywhere. His pace became stronger and faster with every stroke both of us making sounds that was like music to my ears as my orgasm grew closer. My pussy became wetter, my moans grew louder and I threw my girls back at him with so much force, I came all over his dick as he continued to stimulate my clitoris.

*Fuck*, I wanted to yell loud as I could. He was treating my pussy so good that I didn't want him to stop what he was doing until I had another orgasm, but all good things come to an end and I know that, because soon as I was at my peak and ready to cum again, he pulled out of me and came all over my ass. "That was so disrespectful," I stated, looking back at him. He slightly laughed, then grabbed a towel out his desk and wiped my ass, before kissing it. "Thank you," I said, grabbing the same towel and wiping in between my legs before dressing.

I sat in a chair while he sat on his desk letting the silence between us cause the moment to become awkward. I really didn't feel no type of way about fucking him. It was all business, and all part of the game to me, so I quickly took control of the situation.

"I know you're feeling surprised right now, but my pussy comes with a price," I said, really meaning it.

"And what price is that?" he responded quickly. I looked him in the eyes for some kind of sign, because I really didn't know how he would take what I was about to say, but then he met my stare and showed me he was willing to pay whatever the price was.

"Stop fucking with Supreme. I mean, don't sell him nothing, not even an ounce. Loyalty is everything to me and that nigga was disloyal," I said, not feeling an ounce of guilt.

"And I understand that's money you will be missing, so I'll take over his shipment of ten keys at the same price of twenty-two a key," I continued.

He smiled at me, but quickly changed his expression once he saw I was serious.

"I never liked the nigga anyway and I always thought you deserved better. But are you sure you can handle that much work?" he questioned.

"Is a pig's pussy pork? Because last time I checked, it was. I'm one of a kind, like I told you many times before, and I'm not your average bitch. I'll be here in a couple days to pick up my work, so have that ready," I said, then walked out his office with confidence, because I knew I had just become the new H.B.I.C. (Head bitch in charge).

## Chapter Five
### E'mani

I hated the way men like Supreme used women like Mahogany and me. I knew I wasn't the most beautiful woman in the world, but I also knew I deserved to be loved and treated like a woman, and not an animal. Mahogany convinced me to help her give Supreme a dose of his own medicine and I can't lie, I felt real wicked once my mind started racing with ideas.

I called Mrs. Dotson, my realtor, to let her know I was ready to sell my house. Well, I didn't want to. I had to, because of what I had planned for Supreme. I knew he'd be coming here looking for me and I didn't want to be around when he showed up.

"Are you sure that's what you want to do, Ms. Newman? I mean, you just moved in six months ago," she stated. I already had my mind made up and I couldn't change it if I wanted to, but that's something she would never know.

"A lot has happened in the last six months, and I can't live here with memories of the past, so I'm sure. I would also like to know how fast can you find me another house out of Orlando?" I asked. She got quiet for a minute, and then I heard her fumbling through papers before she spoke again.

"Well, Ms. Newman," she started. "I have good news, and bad news, which would you like to hear first?" Just the thought of there being bad news sent chills up my spine. It's always something you would rather live without, that's why it's called bad news.

"Give me the good news first, and then the bad," I said. She spoke again as I continued to listen. "The good news is that I have a beautiful house up for sale in the suburbs of St. Petersburg. Now it's not as big as your current house, but it's posh with four bedrooms, and two and a half bathrooms. And I'm proud to say that it's the former home of entertainers, such as Rick Ross and Trina." She paused for a minute then started again. "Now the bad news is that it might take a couple of months to sell your current home, being that my schedule causes for me to be out of town for the next two months, but far as the house in St. Petersburg, we can get started on the paperwork right away."

That wasn't really bad news, because it didn't matter how long it took to sell the house. I'm just glad I have somewhere else to go. "I'll take it. I trust your taste and quality, so I'm not interested in seeing the house right now, but can you text me the address, and then meet me there in about two hours so we can get everything started with the paperwork?" I said.

We talked for about ten more minutes before I told her I had business to take care of, then hung up.

It was total chaos once I pulled up to my next destination. I saw so many customers coming in and out that it reminded me of a crack house, but minus the neighborhood. I was so nervous as I got out of the car and walked to the front door. A white man held it for me and smiled, letting me know that he's a gentleman. I smiled back before thanking him, because nowadays it was hard to find a man who's a gentleman, let alone somebody who would hold the door for me.

"Welcome to Wells Fargo. How may I assist you today?" a white woman greeted me at the clerk's counter. I reached into my purse, and grabbed all the necessary papers I would need, before explaining to her that I would like to do a withdrawal. She quickly scanned over the documents, then asked for my identification before typing in the account number. From the expression she gave once she pulled up Supreme's account, I knew there was at least six figures in it.

"The account balance is one million dollars. How much do you wish to withdraw today, ma'am?" she asked. I felt like a statue as I stood there amazed, because Supreme never let his accounts reach a million dollars. He would always stop depositing money once he reached five hundred thousand, so I felt like it was meant for me to have his money.

"All of it," I stated, once I gained my composure. She explained to me that she couldn't withdraw over ten thousand dollars, so she would have to call her supervisor. I waited for about five minutes, and then I was greeted by a Mr. Woods, and we proceeded to his office.

"Ok, Ms. Newman. What I'm presenting to you is a contract explaining that if you get robbed once you exit the bank, Wells Fargo is not held responsible. It's the bank's policy that every customer who withdraws ten thousand dollars or more must sign." I signed the contract, along with two more just like it for Supreme's other two accounts, then watched as Mr. Woods looked at my ID card before exiting his office. I took a seat in front of his desk, and grabbed a *U.S. Weekly* magazine, while I waited on my money to show up just to ease my mind a little.

Twenty minutes had passed before Mr. Woods returned with two police officers by his side. I looked up at the two officers and knew they were here to lock me up, and probably throw away the key. I had never been to jail, but I've heard stories about how women got broomsticks and other objects forced up their kitty by other inmates, and that terrified me.

"Relax, Ms. Newman. They're only here to make sure you make it to your car safely with the amount of money you just withdrew," Mr. Woods explained. I relaxed like he suggested, by taking deep breaths to calm my nerves. When I looked up again, I saw for the first time that the second officer was standing behind a cart with hundred-dollar-bills stacked neatly on top of each other. Mr. Woods then grabbed two duffle bags and began filling them up with money, after counting each stack to me carefully, making sure nothing was missing. When every bill was safely inside the bags, the bags were then given to the first officer as we proceeded to my car.

I was living "la vida loca" as I drove my convertible with the top back, and one point five million dollars in my trunk. Pissed off was an understatement to how Supreme would feel once he found out that his money was gone, but who cared, and I wasn't worried about him going to the police, because he's a drug dealer for one and two, he didn't have any proof he obtained that amount of money legally. I knew that for a fact.

It was about two p.m. when I met Mrs. Dotson in St. Petersburg at my soon-to-be new suburban home, and I had to admit, it was breathtakingly beautiful. The; sun was shining just right, giving the house a nice glow, while the pool and basketball court complemented the house's special features. She insisted on giving me a tour, even though I told her she didn't have to. I was buying the house regardless, but I was glad she did, because I fell in love once I laid my eyes on the master bedroom, which had a fourteen-foot ceiling, and windows that were taller than I was.

"What do you think, Ms. Newman?" my realtor asked me.

I was still amazed as I responded to her, "This place is so amazing. When can I move in?"

She flipped through the few papers she held in her arms, then looked up at me with a huge smile on her face. "Right now if you want. All you have to do is sign this piece of paper and have me a check for one hundred and eighty-thousand dollars ready by tomorrow."

I signed the paper faster than lightning, then promised her that she would have her check the next day. When she finally left, I called a moving company to clean out my house in Orlando and told them under no circumstances should they give anybody information about where they're taking it. Then, I disclosed to them that they could find a spare door key under the doormat on the front porch.

*This has been a crazy week for me*, I thought, as I took my shoes off and hugged my plush carpet. I was surprised I didn't have a nervous breakdown from all the stress I had been going through. From Supreme, to Mahogany, and then my mother, I don't know how one person can go through so much, and still keep their head up. But I am a survivor and I owe that to my father, rest in peace.

As I remember, my father Daryl Newman was a smooth, and very respected gentleman. D-New, as everybody outside my family knew him as was full-blooded Jamaican with the sexy swagger of Harold Perrineau. He stood a solid six foot four, had broad shoulders with nice looking dreads hanging down his back.

He was far from a street thug. Matter of fact, he was a successful accountant, which is the main reason I chose the same profession, because I knew that's what he would have wanted. It had been rumored that he was working for this mob family, and wanted to move on to start his own business after ten long years, being that he had witnessed so much he was a threat to the family, and had to be taken care of. My thing is they didn't have to kill him execution-style. Mama and I couldn't even see the body at his funeral, because it had to be a closed casket.

I wiped my face of falling tears from the thought of my father, then called Mahogany to let her in on what all I had accomplished. She answered, but quickly explained to me that she couldn't talk at the moment, and would call me back later. I sat my phone on the floor beside me, and started at the ceiling. I was bored out of this world. I couldn't go to Orlando and check on the progress of the moving company, because I was afraid Supreme might show up, but then again, I didn't even know if he knew his money was missing yet. After a while, I closed my eyes, and fell asleep. I was awakened three hours later by two gentlemen from the moving company. This was the first trip and I have to admit they did an awesome job for four hours of work. Most of my things made it on the first go around, and that really impressed me.

Once they unloaded the truck, and had my thing neatly placed where I wanted them, I tipped them both before sending them on their way until tomorrow. My phone rang, and I let it for a couple of seconds just to hear Alicia Keys' voice. That girl can sing out of this world, and her voice always calmed me down mentally.

"E'mani speaking," I answered in a professional manner.

"Why do you answer the phone like that? You sound so damn lame."

"Excuse me? I was raised to be educated not ghetto, so I use good grammar, not that slang nonsense you talk."

"Don't even go there, because just the other day when I walked in on Supreme eating your pussy, you wasn't talking that proper shit." I wanted to hang up in her face so bad, because she just didn't get it. You can't go around talking to people any kind of way, and think that it's okay. She needed somebody to teach her a lesson, and if I wasn't a woman of God, I would've done it a long time ago.

"Mahogany, why do you always have to use profanity when you talk to people? That's so not ladylike," I stated. She continued to give me a piece of her mind, and again used profanity to add emphasis to her words. I just said forget it, and moved on to another subject, because she wasn't going to change.

"Did Supreme come home yet, or is he still missing in action?" I asked.

"Hell naw, that nigga ain't come home, and if he know what I know, he might not have a home to come to."

"Well, I just want to let you know I did my part, and withdrew every last penny out of every last one of his accounts," I said with confidence. She got quiet for a minute, and all I heard was heavy breathing, like she was trying to catch her breath.

"Mahogany!" I shouted.

"How much money did you get him for?"

"One-point-five million dollars—"

"What? You bullshittin'!" she shouted. Now it was my turn to get quiet, because here she was talking that slang stuff again. I was lost and I didn't know what the hell "bullshittin" meant, so I changed the subject again.

"I bought me a house in St. Petersburg today and decided to drop out of school, because I can't risk Supreme catching up with me."

"Listen, E'mani. I know you might think I'm a ghetto bitch and honestly, I don't give a fuck, but we have to stick together from here on out. That's the only way we can make it without getting hurt or even killed. That was a good decision you made buying a house out of town, but just continue to lay low and I'll keep you posted with what's going on, on my end."

I rolled my eyes at her, happy she wasn't here to see, and we continued to talk, at least until she pissed me off and I hung up on her. I sat on the couch, quiet and afraid at the same time. The realization of what I had gotten myself into had just hit me, and at that moment, I felt nauseous. I needed prayer real bad, and there was only one person I could always count on to give it to me, and that was my mother. I knew I couldn't tell her what I did though, because she was one of them Christians that would make me go in front of the whole congregation, and confess my sins, then ask God for forgiveness. I called her anyway despite how I felt, and her answering machine picked up.

"You have reached the Newman family. Sorry we're not home to take your call right now, but if you would please leave your name, number, and a brief message, we will be sure to get back to you as soon as possible. Thank you, and have a blessed day." Soon as my mother's voice faded and I heard the loud beep indicating the machine had started recording, I spoke nervously stumbling over my words.

"M-M-Ma. It's me. I'm sorry I didn't call you yesterday after church. I don't have an excuse. So I'm not going to make one up, but I have really been going through a lot these last couple of days. I just recently bought a house in St. Petersburg, so that's where I'm living now." I stopped to wipe the tears from my face, not knowing I was crying until I felt something wet hit my arms. "When you get this message, Mama, please call me. Love you!" I sat there for ten minutes, daydreaming with the phone still to my ear once I hung up. I didn't know what else to do and for the first time ever, I felt like a prisoner in my own house.

# Chapter Six
## Mahogany

The word on the streets of Deland was that Supreme had a price on our heads, and when I say our, I mean E'mani and me. I knew that was going to happen once he found out all his money was taken out of his accounts, and that I had left him, taking the whole hundred thousand he had in his safe. That's a lesson for all the ballers in the world, fucking over a bitch like me will only leave you broke and feeling like you got fucked.

I sold his house, which was in my name, for a nice piece of change before moving in with E'mani in St. Pete. We had actually become close over the short time we spent together, and I can't lie, I felt really sorry for her, being that she had to quit school because of me. I know graduating from college was important to her, but we had enough money between the both of us that she could buy another college degree. Lately though, she had become real moody and I knew it wasn't that time of the month, so I wasn't taking that as an excuse from her. Even though she wouldn't admit it, I knew this whole situation was stressing her out, and by me being the stronger of the two, I had to find a solution to our problem.

After two long weeks of taking my mind through a mental roller coaster, I finally had an idea. I figured if I did this right, I could kill two birds with one stone. We needed protection, no questions asked, and I needed the drugs I got from Doe Boy to get sold, so I made a couple phone calls and a couple promises to put everything in play. I put E'mani up on game so she wouldn't be surprised when shit hit the fan and within a week, I felt like a kid in a candy store.

Among E'mani and I were five of the most thorough bitches I knew from back in the day, that were about whatever and ready to get money, so I didn't have a problem with inviting them into our home and introducing everybody.

First, there was Nah Nah. She stood about five foot seven, with peach-colored skin, long jet-black hair down her back, and an ass so phat that she attracted most of the ballers whenever we hung out. She was from Brooklyn, New York, and wasn't a stranger when it came to busting her gun, so we sometimes joked and nicknamed her Shoot'em Up.

Next, there was Nicole. She was the reason most niggas hated to see a bitch in charge. Before her husband got jammed on a twenty-five-to-life bid, she would buy all the coke she could get her hands on in her city, then force all the wannabe ballers to cop from her, and only sell them fourteen grams or less. She stood an even five feet tall, was slightly parrot-toed, and had the strong features of actress Kyla Pratt. She was born in Largo, Florida, but grew up in the slums of Palm Beach.

Then, there were the twins, Coco and Shanel. Even though they were identical, they were different as night and day. Coco was always the sassy, stuck up, "I know I'm the shit so watch your man" type. Shanel came off as the loyal, independent ride or die chick. They both were a small five foot two, with a petite frame, but their unique background of Hawaiian, Korean, and African American is what made them stand out. They were born in Hawaii, but were raised in Panama City, Florida.

Last, but not least, there was Kayla. She was from Jacksonville, Florida. So that meant she didn't have a problem cut throating any nigga, bitch, dog or cat. She was one of them bitches that would fuck her mother's husband if it meant she would get something other than a wet ass. She stood about five foot seven, her skin was the color of rich chocolate, and she had the body of a *Straight Stuntin' Magazine* model. I used to tell her she always reminded me of Buffie the Body, but with a cuter face.

We all gave each other hugs, and it made me smile because the Baller Babies were reunited. It had been five years since we first met each other at Florida Institution for Teenage Girls in 2013. Real recognized real, so we all clicked up like a MAC-11 without bullets, and from there, we formed the Baller Babies. We all had one thing in common, and that was money. So despite our situation, we weren't going to let anybody stop us from getting

I showed Nah Nah and Nicole to their rooms, while Coco, Shanel, and Kayla took the couches. I then told them to get themselves together, and meet me in the game room in two hours. We had business to discuss. Two hours came so fast that it shocked me, because I was still putting together my speech when the girls walked in. They all sat quiet at the round table, waiting on me to tell them their next move.

"Like I told you all on the phone, I'm in some deep shit and I need your help," I started. "I know you all remember Supreme. Well, he did some disrespectful and disloyal shit, and now we're beefin'. So far I've took all his money and took over his connect. I have plenty work for y'all, so when you're ready let me know and to show my appreciation, if you would look under your seats, there is twenty grand for all of you. With that said, does anybody have any questions?" They all checked their seats and their faces lit up when they saw the money. Even though that was a lot of money I just gave away, I smiled, because they were going to make us twice as much.

"Mahogany, girl, you know we got your back. It's the Baller Babies to the end. We were there for each other then, and we gone be there for each other now, so what's understood don't need to be explained," Nah Nah said, withdrawing her pistol.

"Damn, Shoot'em Up. You still got that old ass .380. Girl, you haven't changed one bit," Nicole shouted as everybody burst into laughter. It felt good to be around my girls again. They understood me, went through what I went through, and they always showed a bitch that sista love.

A week later, they all surprised me by moving out and buying a five-bedroom house in Deland. They said they were ready to get things going and make their own money. I didn't have a problem with that. I just hoped they were careful and knew what they were doing, because Deland was Supreme's turf. E'mani overheard everything and went into panic mode. She knew what Supreme was capable of, and didn't want to see the girls get hurt, but what she didn't know was that Nah Nah, Nicole, Coco, Shanel, and Kayla were just as dangerous, and that the Baller Babies were a force to be reckoned with.

I FedEx'ed the girls their packages, and watched from afar while they worked their magic. I had faith in them. I just hoped Nah Nah and Kayla wouldn't let their tempers get in the way or temporarily blind them from getting money.

The next fourteen to fifteen days, I stayed home and relaxed while my young gun, T.J. occasionally came by to give me updates on how the Baller Babies were slowly taking Deland by surprise in the drug trade. I never told T.J. I was the head of the Baller Babies, so he thought he was just getting paid to tell me whose names were ringing in the streets of Deland. And that's how I liked it.

I pulled my cell phone out to call Nicole, because tonight I felt like celebrating the Baller Babies' success in Deland. Fuck how Supreme felt. If we bumped into each other, then it is what it is.

"What's up, bitch?" Nicole answered on the second ring.

"I hear the Baller Babies makin' niggas shut down shop, because they can't make no money?"

"You damn right, and we hiring if they need a job," she replied, and we both burst into laughter.

"Girl, you a trip. Listen though. I was thinking tonight we shut down early, and hit up that club downtown, and ball like we're known for doing," I suggested.

"Deland or St. Pete?"

"Deland, bitch! It's time we let the city know why we're called the Baller Babies," I replied excitedly. I'm sure Nicole felt how I felt so it was all up to Coco, Shanel, Nah Nah, and Kayla, and knowing them, they weren't letting us go out by ourselves so the Baller Babies was ballin' out tonight.

"Well meet us at Club Paid at about nine," Nicole said.

"Club Paid at nine. I'll be there. Bye, bitch," I shot back, then hung up.

I pulled up to Club Paid at about 9:15 in E'mani's silver Lexus, and all eyes were on me. I couldn't tell you what year or model it was, but I knew I looked good driving it. I didn't see the girls as I looked around, so that meant they were probably already in the club having a good time. I walked in, and was damn near blinded from so many bright lights, but I had to give the owner his props, whoever he was, because this place was decked out like I've never seen before. Upon entering, a red carpet was laid out while cameras flashed everywhere, giving you a little taste of a Hollywood event. I was far from one of them skinny ass model bitches, but you couldn't tell me nothing as I sashayed down the red carpet like I was on a runway. I grilled the cameras, showing all six of my gold teeth, and occasionally blew kisses to give them a little taste of my feminine side. Damn, I was a bad bitch, and it seemed like the older I got, the sexier I became. I waved at all the people I knew and ignored all the catcalls, until this one dude caught my attention, stopping me in mid-stride.

"You know they say that ass fake from the way it's shaped, but I ain't gone lie. I still like it." I turned to face him, and decided to play his little game as I walked to his table.

"You want this pussy. Don't you?" I asked in a flirtatious manner.

He licked his thick lips, then sat up in his chair before responding. "Damn right, I want it."

"Well, first I gotta know. Have you ever been lucky enough to receive your red wings?"

He stared at me with a twisted look and I could tell he was lost.

"I see you don't understand what I'm talking about, so I'll put it like this," I said, then slid out of my jeans and panties, before propping my leg up next to his face and pulling off my maxi pad, watching as blood poured slowly down my leg. "I like my kisses down low."

"Bitch!" he snapped, standing up in my face but before he could finish his sentence, Nah Nah appeared from out of nowhere, with her gun pressed to his temple like a trained assassin.

"Sit yo ass down," she demanded, and the look in his eyes was evidence of his fear as he obeyed. "You have two choices. Now you can calm yo ass down and chill, or we can start shooting it out in this bitch and long as I get you, I don't care if I get stamped or not." He quietly chose option number one and headed to the bar, almost falling face first as he tripped over his own legs.

Nah Nah and I both burst out laughing until tears formed at the corner of our eyes. After having our little fun, it was time the Baller Babies turned up and let everybody know why we were called the Baller Babies. I whispered in Nah Nah's ear, then watched as she walked towards the huge bar to handle business. She swiftly eased through body after body and within seconds, she was back by my side handing me a cordless microphone. I cleared my throat and when I had everybody's attention, I made my announcement.

"I hate to be the bitch of bad news, but the Baller Babies just bought out the whole bar and if you ain't no bitch, it's best you find another club to go to, because you will not be drinking in here tonight!"

The whole club went quiet as most of the men stared at each other before parting like the Red Sea, and walking out the door. I swear I thought that I was the reason for it, but once I turned to face Nah Nah, I knew that wasn't the case. She reminded me of a cocked pistol, dangerously powerful, and you had no choice but to respect her.

Once everybody was back to having a good time. I peeped at Kayla, and saw her shifting in the booth she was in. She hated the club scene, she really did. Hated having so many bodies so close to hers. Hated the noise, the smell, everything. I couldn't imagine how my girl felt being out of her environment like she was, so I had to go comfort her.

"What's up, you having a good time?" I asked, knowing she probably wasn't.

"Yeah, I'm cool. I was just waiting on a friend, that's it. Why you ask?"

I wanted to tell her that she was lying about having a good time, but I held my tongue and smiled. "I was just checking up on my girl you know how we roll, but I'm about to go shake my ass on that fine ass brother right there, after getting him a drink."

Oh yeah, I forgot to mention only the men who considered themselves as boss statues stayed in the club, and I had to respect that, because it was basically self-explanatory. I proceeded to the bar, and ordered two drinks, then found my dance partner for the night after temporarily losing him. We danced the whole night, and I could literally say unlike most men, he was handling every last bit of this forty-inch ass I was throwing on him. We then ended the night with a friendly competition to see who would run out of money first, making it rain to Boosie Badazz's "Bankroll."

## "Coco"

The sound of Dipset screaming through the surround sound speakers woke me from one of the most erotic dreams I've ever had. And it was an understatement to say that I was pissed off. I looked to my left, checking the alarm clock on my dresser, then put my head back under the covers, because I wanted to stamp Nah Nah for having that damn music up so loud. She knew damn well that everybody in the house had a hangover, and was recovering from last night's events at Club Paid. After ten minutes of trying to get back to my dream and failing, I threw a long t-shirt over my naked body and dragged myself out of bed. "Nah Nah, what the fuck is wrong with you, playing that damn music while everybody trying to sleep?" I shouted on my way to the living room. My head was hurting, and I didn't give a damn about lashing out at her at the moment. But I was soon stopped in my tracks when I got there, and feeling like a spooked cat as I scanned the room.

"About time you woke your ass up, Sleeping Beauty," Shanel stated as laughter filled the room. Everybody was already up eating breakfast, and nobody thought to wake me up to see if I was hungry. I mugged every last one of them with a plate in their hand making sure they saw what kind of mood I was in. Before I could open my mouth though, they all pointed towards the kitchen, while Shanel shouted over the music that my plate was in the oven. I couldn't even keep the unit on my face as I turned on the heels of my feet, and went back to my room. I wanted to be mad at somebody so bad, but nobody gave me a reason to be. I jumped in the shower, brushed my teeth and got dressed, before doing my hair and throwing on a little makeup. I then grabbed a couple buds of loud from out my stash, a Swisher Sweet, and went on the front porch to enjoy the cool breeze.

While some females like to start their days chasing behind men, and trying to trap them with babies, I like to start mine off getting high or getting my pussy ate, and since I didn't have a golden head at the time, blowing smoke was the next best thing. Free smoke, free smoke!

I was halfway through my blunt and feeling like I was halfway to heaven, when I heard a deep voice that made my pussy vibrate. My eyes shot open and I couldn't help but stare at the man in front of me, with skin the color of a Twix candy bar and waves so deep in his head, I swear I almost drowned just from looking at them.

"You enjoying yourself in my city?" he asked with a smile. I could tell he had no idea who he was talking to, but I never forget a face, and since he was lost, I decided to follow him until he was found or found out who he was talking to.

"Yo city?" I stated, "The last time I checked, Donald Trump won the presidential votes for Florida, so how can this be your city?"

He burst into laughter before extending his hand to me, "Now that was funny. My name's Supreme."

"Mine's Baller Baby," I shot back, shaking his hand. His eyes became wide as his grip on my hand became tighter. It was clear that I had caught him by surprise and damn near three minutes passed before he released my hand.

"You the one that's been flooding my city with that bullshit you selling. You've cost me a lot of money. You know that?"

"That's my job, and by the way, Mahogany and E'mani sent their love," I stated with a smile. From the mention of their names Supreme went into a rage, and within a blink of an eye, he was brandishing a black semi-automatic handgun. My heart started beating rapidly at the first sight of it, but I kept my composure, afraid to let him see the fear he caused in me and smiled like I was in a portrait with the first family. "Let the war begin," I stated, not expecting it, but happy as hell she showed up.

Shoot'em came up out the house busting her gun at that exact moment, sending bullets flying everywhere. All I could think about was the money we would be missing, because we damn sure wouldn't be able to open up shop today after what just happened.

## Chapter Seven
### Supreme

I was drenched in sweat, and my lungs felt like they were about to explode as I tried to catch my breath breathing in air at lightning speed. I couldn't believe a bitch just tried to stamp me. What the hell was going on, and to make matters worse, I didn't even know who the chick was. I checked my waistband for my gun, and cursed myself when I didn't feel it, because I knew I had dropped it in my attempt to escape getting shot. I paced my living room floor for thirty minutes trying to figure out something, and then it hit me.

Ever since them Baller Baby bitches came on the scene, it's like that's when the problems started, and then I remembered the chick today said something about Mahogany and E'mani, two bitches that were at the top of my list to kill. They were the reason my connect, Doe Boy stopped fucking with me, and then they took all my damn money, forcing me to borrow money from my main man, just so I could pay for this bullshit ass coke I was getting from my new Spanish connect, Baby King. Something kept telling me that Mahogany and E'mani were working together with them Baller Baby bitches, and if that was the case, then they better have a good defense, because we about to have court in the streets. I made a couple of phone calls to the workers I had pushing my drugs. I needed all of them to be on the lookout, but I knew something had to be wrong when not one of them answered their phones.

"Damn!" I shouted, not realizing that I was thinking out loud. I ran into my room, grabbed my .45 from underneath my bed, then headed back out the door, barely making it to my ride. I ran right into a parade of police officers, cuffing and loading every last one of my workers in a paddy wagon. "What the fuck is going on around here?" I asked, thinking out loud again.

"Give me a dollar, and I'll tell you," said a faint voice.
I looked to my right where I heard the tiny voice come from, and shook my head. Lil Man Man, the son of a crackhead was out here

with no shoes, no shirt, and snot from his nose hanging damn near to his bottom lip. I hated to see kids like this, and his daddy probably was disclaiming him, because he already had a wife and kids when he went out tricking and made Lil Man Man. I reached in my pocket, pulling out a five-dollar-bill, and handed it to him, while I listened to him talk.

"Them pretty girls down the street was shooting, and one shot Hollywood in the shoulder. Mrs. Lynn called the police, and by the time they showed up, everybody still had their guns out so they took them to jail—"

"Man Man, brang your lil' nappy head ass here," his mom yelled, slapping him in the back of his head. "What I told you about being in grown folks' business? If anybody ask, you tell them you haven't seen a damn thing. I don't care who it is. Now get yo lil' bad ass in the house before I go get my belt."

I slightly laughed as Man Man started crying, and ran into the house. I couldn't blame his mother for saying what she said. He might end up telling the wrong person what he saw, and they put a bullet in his little head for being a witness. When it's a life on the life, people these days didn't care how young the witnesses were, they had to go.

"How the fuck am I going to do that?" I said to myself, now feeling like I was going crazy. I mean I had a feeling that Mahogany and E'mani were the head, but how can I kill them if I didn't know where to find them.

I rushed to my room, thinking I heard a female voice, but found it empty when I got there. Damn, I was losing my mind, I thought, as I sat on the end of my bed. I looked around the room not expecting to find anything, but a small object on my nightstand caught my attention. I reached across my bed to grab it, because I hadn't remembered putting it there, and caught myself staring at it longer than I intended to. It was a picture of E'mani and me in the Virgin Islands. She looked so beautiful, and then at that moment, a plan popped into my head. I rushed to my phone almost missing numbers as I dialed, and waited until I heard a familiar voice.

"The Newman residence. This is Mrs. Newman. How may I help you?"

"How are you, Mrs. Newman? This is E'mani's boyfriend, Supreme, and I was wondering if you had E'mani's new address?"

## Chapter Eight
### E'mani

I had just come home from working out at the gym downtown. I was tired, exhausted, and my body felt slick from sweating. All I wanted to do was take a shower, and get into my bed, and be dead to the world. I walked to the front door to unlock it, and was surprised to see it was ajar. I yelled out for Mahogany, thinking maybe she forgot to close the door when she came into the house, but I never received a response. I slowly eased my way in and walked into the kitchen.

Nothing. Everything looked normal. I then walked upstairs just to make sure everything was how I left it, but the closer I got the more confused I became, because I didn't remember leaving the stereo on in my room. I walked close enough to the door to where I could put my ear to it, and listened, and all I heard was Alicia Keys' smoothing voice. Without hesitation, I grabbed the doorknob and slowly pushed the door open to catch whoever was in my room by surprise, but again, everything looked normal. I laughed at myself for being so scary, and walked over to my dresser to turn off the stereo. *I don't know where I get being so scary from*, I thought, and laughed again. Soon as I turned around to get in my closet, I was stopped dead in my tracks with my voice caught in my throat, because I couldn't scream as bad as I wanted to. Supreme was here in my room with a look that scared the hell out of me on his face.

"Please don't hurt me," I pleaded.

"Take off your clothes."

"No...Supreme, please don't do this," I continued to beg.

He then withdrew a nickel-plated gun, and just the sight of the cold steel made me want to scream, but I was too afraid. "Take off your clothes now, and this is the last time I'm going to tell you," he demanded.

My tears started to temporarily blur my vision, and I slowly undressed myself until I was naked as the day I came into this world. He forced me onto my bed, and I shut my eyes tight as I felt him lay next to me.

"Please don't do this...please," I pleaded again, but it was like my pleas fell on deaf ears. After a minute, I felt his hands caressing my breasts, my nipples, then he moved slowly down my body until he reached my thighs. He stayed there for a while and I hate to admit it, but I was getting turned on from the way he touched me. I moaned my satisfaction and he surprised me by forcefully inserting two of his fingers inside my kitty, making me gasp for air. The pain quickly turned to pleasure, and I continued to moan as he sexed me and stimulated my clitoris with his fingers, bringing me closer and closer to reaching my peak. I was almost there and I knew he could tell from my heavy breathing. He pumped his fingers in and out of me faster and I screamed I was cumming. I was ready. I felt it. Without further warning, I released at that moment, and at the same exact time I felt Supreme's teeth lightly pulling on my clitoris.

"Ahhhhh!" I yelled at the top of my lungs, loving the way my body was feeling.

"E'mani," I heard him say my name, but I couldn't open my eyes.

"I want more," was all I could reply.

"E'mani!" he said again, this time shouting.

"I want more!" I shouted back.

"E'mani!"

"Give me more!

"E'mani!... girl, wake your ass up!" I heard as I felt my body being shaken wildly. My eyes shot open and I was drenched in sweat as Mahogany stood over me in my bed. "Girl, you alright? I don't know what kind of dream you were having, but I could hear you screaming all the way from my room."

My heart was beating like a bass drum, and all I could think about was how embarrassed I felt at that moment. Did she hear me scream I want more or did she hear me moan? I looked at her so I could get a hint from her body language, but all she did was stare at me looking clueless of what to say. I had to know if she knew, so I tested the waters to try to see what she heard. "It felt so real. Supreme was trying to kill me."

"How? By fucking you to death?" she laughed, then continued. "It seems to me that you were enjoying it, because all I remember hearing is, I' want more, give me more,'" she mocked, and continued to laugh as she walked out of my room.

I sat on my bed, painting my toenails while I waited for my curling iron to heat up. I had a big day ahead of me. First I had to go by the health department to get my six-month check-up, something my mother had always made me do ever since I was sixteen, because she found out that I was having sex. While I was there, I had to get on contraception. I laughed at myself as I thought about what I called a big day. I really didn't have that much to do, but I didn't know how long I would have to sit, and wait in the health department. It took fifteen minutes, but the curling iron finally got hot enough to where I could curl my hair to perfection, and continue turning myself into a diva. I checked myself one last time in the mirror, and then proceeded on my way once I was satisfied. I stopped by Mahogany's room on my way out just to see what she was up to, even though I knew she would laugh at me, because of the dream I had earlier, but I didn't care.

"What you doing?" I asked, catching her by surprise. She jumped, then quickly hid the book from my sight like I never saw it.

"Is that a Lexicon you reading?"

"No, get out of my room," she shouted, trying to force me out the door.

"Hold up," I stated. "Answer this question for me, and then I'll leave. Why are so many black people so ashamed to learn, but never ashamed to be ignorant?" She just stared at me without saying a word until I walked off.

I had begun to know St. Pete quite well, so within twenty minutes of getting in my car, I was less than two blocks from the health department. The parking lot was full of cars when I did get there, and I really felt that I was going to be here all day, because it took me ten full minutes just to find a parking spot. I knew that had to be a sign. After I safely parked my baby without getting her scratched up, I strutted to the door, and then took a deep breath before opening it, and going in.

*OmiGod*, I thought as I scanned the whole place with my eyes. There were so many people in here that I could have sworn they were having a sale on prescription medication. I walked to the receptionist's desk to check in before finding me a seat, which was almost impossible. There were people everywhere, most of them were women with kids, and then there were a group of five men dressed in women clothes. They received most of the attention, because they were going back and forth with each other about whose backside and breasts looked more realistic.

My mind was focused on the two girls sitting opposite them, though I knew it wasn't polite to stare, I couldn't help but wonder how young they both were. The one with the lighter complexion and designer glasses on her face looked like she couldn't have been older than twenty-one. The other girl looked young too, but her body was more filled out so I would give her about twenty-three.

After a minute or so, their names were called. And they got up to follow the doctor, while I pulled a novel by Wahida Clark out of my purse and started reading where I'd left off. Every five to ten minutes, I would check my watch to see how much time had passed since I'd arrived, and after twenty-five minutes, I closed my book and placed it back in my purse. My eyes were hurting and I had to use the ladies room. Soon as I stood to go, the door to the doctor's offices opened and both girls emerged, hugging each other and crying like their whole world had been turned upside down. I stared as they walked to the back of the waiting area, eyes puffy and red. Something kept telling me to go comfort them and I knew that was my mother's blood in me, but I fought the urge, because I didn't know either of them. I fixed my clothes, before proceeding to the ladies' room, and I couldn't stop myself as I kept walking until I was face-to-face with both girls.

"I don't know what happened in there today to have you two so upset, but always remember God still loves you, and he does have a plan for the both of your lives." Both girls stared at me, and I could tell they weren't sure what to say, so I said again, "He still loves you."

Once they looked at each other again, I guess figuring I wasn't armed or dangerous, they both hugged me, and just broke down letting everything out. They introduced themselves as Ashlyn and Alice once I told them my name and then they explained to me the reason they were so upset.

"OmiGod!" was all I could muster before I grabbed their hands and started praying, not caring how loud I was. Prayer wouldn't undo their situation, but it would help them deal with it, and feel better about it. Soon as we finished and said amen, the doctor was calling my name. I hugged them both, then excused myself. This wasn't my regular doctor, so I had to explain to him what my normal visits consist of. He shook his head, grabbed my chart, and scanned it before going to work, making the whole process look easier than my doctor usually did. I was happy that everything took no longer than twenty minutes, and soon as I received my contraception, I was on my way. I was so ready to go, I almost didn't hear Ashlyn and Alice, trying to get my attention.

"We want to thank you for praying for us, because despite our situation, you really did make us feel better. If you ever need anything, here's my number. Our dad's rich, so don't be afraid to ask," Ashlyn said, once we were face-to-face. I thanked both girls while I programmed the number into my phone and then hugged them once again, before turning to leave.

I drove home wondering if Mahogany had spilled the beans to the girls about my dream, and her having to wake me up. Yeah, the Baller Babies were back together, and everybody can thank Supreme for that. They had moved back in a couple days ago after finding out from watching the news that their house had been shot up. There were so many holes in their house, you would have thought the whole neighborhood used it for target practice. All in all though, I couldn't complain, because it felt kind of good to have company, and whenever we're all together we have nothing but fun.

"Suwoo....Blatt!" was all I heard upon entering the house. I had no idea what it was, and it seemed like the closer I came to the living room, the louder it got.

"Suwoo...Blatt!" I heard it once again, and soon as I emerged from the kitchen, I saw Nah Nah with a red bandanna over her mouth, and another one on her right wrist. She was throwing up gang signs while Kayla videotaped her on the camcorder.

"What are you doing, and why are you making so much noise?" I asked, still looking confused as I watched Nah Nah twist her fingers.

"I'm sending a video to my homies back home in New York. You know the blood got that shit sewed up over there, and if you ain't banging that five, you ain't gone survive, Suwoo...Blatt!" she screamed at me before laughing.

I didn't know anything about gangs and to be honest, I didn't want to know. I went to my room, kicked off my shoes, and soon as I laid my head on my feather soft pillow, I was out, sleeping like a stone. The sound of my ringing phone blasting in my ear woke me up about an hour before I really wanted to wake up. I was sleeping too good and once I checked the time, I realized I had only been asleep for an hour and thirty minutes, so I was not happy.

"Hello?" I answered in a sluggish tone, hoping my caller caught the hint that I was tired, and let me go back to sleep.
"I see you've been playing hooky from church for the last couple of weeks, you know God don't like that. He wants his time."

"How are you, Mama? And I haven't been playing hooky. I just been busy," I shot back, once I realized who it was. Mama didn't care what you had going on in your life. Every Sunday was God's day and to her, it was a sin if you didn't show up to church.

"Too busy for God, huh? Don't worry, he see everything, but the reason I called is to let you know that someone called the house for you about three days ago," she said.
"What's their name?"
"Oh, let me think. Sudean? Supreme? Supreme. That was it. He

said he was your boyfriend, and he wanted to know if I would give him your new address," she replied.

I felt like I was going to faint and at that moment, my life felt like a horror movie. What was Supreme trying to do? Send me a message by bringing my mother into this? I hope that wasn't the case.

"Ma, I hope you didn't tell him?" I said when I finally got my voice back.

"E'mani, now you know I wouldn't do that. I might be old, but I'm not dumb. I told him if you wanted him to have your address, you would have given it to him," she shot back.

I talked with my mother for about thirty more minutes, careful not to let it show in my voice that I was scared, and someone was trying to hurt me. I did a good job at it and she finally hung up, but I couldn't find the number fast enough as I searched through my contacts and found Ashlyn's. I hated to call in my favor so early, but Supreme had to be taken care of. He crossed the line when he called my mother, and then look what he did to the girls' house. Excuse my French, but his ass was grass.

## Chapter Nine
### Mahogany

"Mmmm-hmmmm! Eat this pussy, baby, eat it." I was feeling so much pleasure as I got my pussy ate something serious, by the same street thug Nah Nah had to pull her gun on that night we balled out in Club Paid. I didn't even know his name, but his sexy swagger, and confidence was a turn-on for me and I needed this stress reliever. I was on my hands and knees, with my legs slightly spread apart when the head started feeling so good that I was talking without actually knowing what I was saying.

"I want you to stick your tongue in my ass," I moaned. He looked at me confused, and I grabbed his dreads to push his face between my cheeks, "Do it!" I shouted. I knew he was probably feeling like a little bitch, but fuck 'em. You gotta know how to handle a bitch like me. He slowly licked his tongue around my hole, then without warning pushed it inside me. I wanted to scream. The feeling was so good that I passed gas without knowing it, soon as I relaxed my muscles.

"What's that smell?" he asked, looking like he swallowed a lemon. I was so embarrassed, all I could do was give him a look that said he was fucking up my groove, and that was enough to get him back to pleasing me. After I came for the second time, I dressed, and sent him on his way. We had been fucking around ever since the night I met him at Club Paid, and he had always pleased me by giving me that golden head and pounding on this pussy, but today, I wasn't in the mood to be around him any longer.

While E'mani was gone to her appointment, and the rest of the girls were asleep, I finally had a chance to sneak him out the house. None of them knew about our relationship and that's how I wanted to keep it. While he was getting dressed, I occasionally peeped out the door to make sure no one was out there. I had to be careful. E'mani had almost caught me earlier before she left. While she thought I was jumping because she scared me, or I didn't want her to see the book I had, that was far from the real reason. I was playing with his dick under the covers and it was by the grace of God I heard her a second before she saw me. We crept through the house like two teenagers who had just broke their curfew, scared that their parents might be sitting up waiting on them. Nah Nah was a light sleeper, and this was one of them days I was mad her room was next to mine. We made it past the game room, then through the kitchen and out the door. I stayed on the front porch as I watched his car pull off, then disappear. Soon as it was out of sight, the front door flew open, almost making me fall through the threshold.

"Who that was you just had in here?" Nah Nah asked.

I was still trying to catch my balance before I hit the floor but I couldn't, so I grabbed her shirt, bringing her down with me. We both laughed until I thought about what she had just said.

"Haven't yo' mama ever told you to stay out of grown folks' business?" I shot back sarcastically. "So touch your nose." She looked at me, then sucked her teeth before getting up and walking back to her room. I knew Nah Nah wasn't afraid of me, but I was more of the big sister of the Baller Babies, so she respected me.

After I got up off the floor myself and brushed the dirt off my ass, I went to the bathroom to take a hot shower. It wasn't long after I got out of the shower that my cell phone started ringing. I was still in my birthday suit feeling free as a bird, and I really didn't feel like being fucked up with anybody. I let it ring until it stopped, then laid on my bed with my legs spread wide, giving my pussy a chance to breathe. Yeah, I did this every once and a while to lower my chance of getting an infection. My doctor told me I had a high risk of catching a yeast infection because my vagina always stayed so moist. I was a nympho, a freak by nature. What did he expect?

I threw on my True Religion blouse and some black spandex with no panties. My clear pumps complemented my pedicured feet, and my fair rested on my shoulders as if it was exhausted. Once I checked the mirror, seeing the baddest bitch since Trina staring back at me, I grabbed my purse and cell phone before walking out the door. My cell phone started ringing again, and I didn't have to check the screen to know that it was Doe Boy calling. I had a specific ringtone for everybody in my contacts, so I knew who was calling soon as it rang. Mad that he didn't catch the hint earlier when I didn't answer that I didn't want to talk over the phone, I let it ring once again until it went to voicemail. When I made it outside, I jumped in my Beamer, driving all the way to Atlanta. It was about that time I hollered at Doe Boy. I needed a small favor anyway.

The parking lot was vacant as it always was in the middle of the day, so I made the familiar visit to the front door to Magic City and within seconds, it magically opened.

"You told me you could handle the work if I let you take over his shipment. Lately, I've been seeing otherwise, and I'm not too happy about that money I'm losing," Doe Boy said soon as we were face-to-face. He was so close, I could smell the vodka on his breath and without answering, I grabbed his hand, and wasted no time rushing to his office.

"I need you," I demanded, breathing heavy while fumbling with his belt. I knew the power a pussy possessed, and I was one of the rare bitches that knew how to use it, so like my mother had taught me years ago, I was about to use what I had to get what I wanted.

Once I had his manhood released from its confinement, Doc Boy forced himself down my throat causing me to gag, almost throwing up my insides. I responded quickly by pushing his back to the wall, then continued deep throating him, while sucking his sack into my mouth at the same time in order to take back control. His soft moans encouraged me to go harder, and at that moment I blacked out, going crazy as my sexual appetite exploded.

An hour later, I came back to my senses and found myself laid out on the floor exhausted. My nipples were throbbing and feeling like they had been bitten by a thousand men and my pussy was so sore, I could barely close my legs without pain shooting through my body like electricity.

"How you feeling over there?" Doe Boy asked once he saw the expression of pain on my face.

"Weak and sorer than a woman who just gave birth to a ten-pound baby. What the hell did you do to me?"

He laughed before licking his thick lips. "Naw, I ain't do shit. You did everything. A woman had never got me so open to where she let me put my tongue in every hole she had before replacing it with my dick. Shawty, you something serious."

I didn't know if I should be proud of myself or what, because he was flattering me with his compliments, but I was not planning on doing what I did. I was just supposed to give him some pussy, that's it. I found my clothes and got dressed before turning to face him. His sexy smile eased the pain a little and before I knew it, he embraced me, and stuck his tongue in my mouth.

"Hold up!" I said, pushing him a little. "I need a favor."

He looked me in the eyes for a second, then slowly asked. "What is it you need?"

"It's Supreme, he's become a problem and the reason why I can't get rid of the work like I did in the beginning. I need him gone," was all I said.

"Well, it's about time. I was wondering when you was gone ask. Consider it done. Ain't nothing worse than having somebody close to you take your life away."

I was in pain the entire drive home. It was a little after eleven p.m. when I pulled up to my house. I was hoping everybody would be asleep to avoid conversation, and them drilling me with questions about where I'd been all day. I knew they meant well, but I was too sore, and not in the mood for their company. I eased out of my car in attempt to sneak into the house, but was suddenly stopped by the excruciating pain to my backside. My ass felt like it was on fire. *What the fuck did he do to me*, I thought as I leaned up against the side of my car to catch my balance. I was in so much pain that I wanted to cry like a baby right there where I stood. I stripped out of all my clothes and moaned when the cool breeze tackled my entire body, especially in between my legs and ass cheeks. I felt like laying on the ground for hours, but I didn't want to catch an indecent exposure or any other kind of sex charge, if by chance the police happened to show up.

All the lights in the house were off, except for the kitchen when I crept in. My intentions were to leave it that way, until I bumped my pinky toe against the corner of the couch, bringing out the lioness in me as I roared. It seemed like every light in the house was turned on as I stood there like a little girl who had just witnessed her puppy get run over by an eighteen-wheeler truck. Yeah, this was definitely an "oh, shit!" moment.

Kayla was on my couch, bumping pussy with another woman, and didn't even try to stop when she noticed I was watching her. All of a sudden, I started feeling nauseous and wanted to throw up at the sight of them two locked together like crabs. This was definitely too much for my young eyes. The situation became worse when Nah Nah showed up seeing ass, pussy, and titties everywhere, as all three of us stood naked as Eve before she ate from the Tree of Knowledge.

## Chapter Ten
### Supreme

I seriously thought this war with them Baller Baby bitches was gone cost me to use all my resources, but little did I know, them bitches wasn't even ready for this beef shit. It had been two weeks since I left their house looking like Swiss cheese, and they hadn't showed their faces in the city. I don't know if that was a good thing or bad, but I knew this, I wasn't sleeping on them. I still hadn't come up with another plan after my last one failed. Yeah Mrs. Newman's old ass didn't want to give me E'mani's new address. I swear, I wanted to drive to her house and burn that muthafucka to the ground, but I respected old people and my heart wasn't that cold. I knew nine times out of ten though, she probably called E'mani, and told her, but she was one person I really wasn't worried about. E'mani was, and always had been a goody-two-shoes church girl, who wouldn't even curse without apologizing to everybody within ear distance.

"Supreme! You listening to what I'm saying, bruh?" Hollywood asked, and I could tell from his tone it wasn't the first time he'd asked me.

"Yeah, I'm listening," I responded. I had bailed Hollywood and the rest of my crew out of jail three days after the shootout. They were all charged with possession of a firearm, so ten percent of their bond was only a thousand dollars apiece. Hollywood told me everything that happened and come to find out, Lil Man Man was telling the truth. Hollywood did get shot, and he was recovering pretty good. Now he was sitting on my couch, telling me about some bitch he met at Club Paid a couple weeks ago.

"Bruh, I swear that this bitch is badder than any bitch you ever had, and she's an in-house freak. One thing I don't like about her though is the way she always want a nigga to eat her pussy before she let me fuck. Talking about she like her kisses down low."

I sat up on the couch and gave Hollywood my full attention. I knew I wasn't trippin', but that last comment sounded too familiar.

"Bruh, how you said your new chick looked again?" I asked as if he had told me already.

"I told you, she badder than any bitch you ever had," he responded, slightly laughing then closed his eyes and gave me a full description of her, like he was mentally looking at a picture. "She got a mixture between a caramel and chocolate skin complexion. She got shoulder-length black hair, money-green eyes, and six gold teeth at the bottom of her mouth. Now tell me she don't sound badder than a bitch."

I continued to listen and tried not to let it show how excited I was, because this had to be who I thought it was. It was just too big of a coincidence. "Bruh, tell me your lil' bitch name is not Mahogany?" I asked, holding my breath as I waited on him to answer. He paused for a quick second and I could clearly see the surprise on his face, but then he looked me in the eyes before smirking at me and stated, "Naw bruh, that ain't her name."

I drove around with my mind wandering like a lost puppy, after I dropped Hollywood's lying ass off on the block so he could get on his grind and make me some money. I knew the bitch he was talking about was Mahogany, but knowing my background he probably thought I'm trying to take her from him, so he didn't want to admit that was her. But money talk and bullshit walk, so I knew for the right price Hollywood would tell me everything I needed to know about her.

While I stopped by a couple of my spots to pick up some money I bobbed my head to some of Lil Boosie Badazz's old songs, being that they were playing all throwback joints on the radio today. I couldn't help but sing along as I knew most of the words, and I felt the energy of the excitement in my body. "I walked outside, I'm tired of this man / my juvy in the yard with draws in her hand / my girl looked at me, and said you dog ass nigga / I'm finna put this knife in your muthafuckin' liva!"

After a couple minutes, the song went off, and I heard the owner of Club Paid broadcasting that tonight he was throwing an all-white party. "Everybody drinks free until midnight, and women get in free all night," he said. I turned down the radio, and headed home to get fresh. I figured I would go to give my mind a break from thinking about all the problems a nigga was going through. Really, to be honest with myself, I think this party might do me some justice. I can't remember when the last time I hung out, and just enjoyed myself.

Now, I couldn't say that I was the richest dude in the club, but I knew it would be a sin to say that I wasn't one of the flyest. I stepped through the double doors of Club Paid looking fresher than a canned good in my all-white Levis, and Polo button-down collared shirt. I even had on the Polo White cologne, just enough to make the women do a double take when they smelled my scent. And to top everything off, my waves were on swim tonight, and looking extra deep from the Murray I blessed them with.

I received my VIP pass from the bouncer at the door, and continued on my way as I passed DJ Pinky P at the spin table. She smiled at me, and then got on the mic to announce that I was in the building. I felt like royalty as dudes dapped me up and women gave me hugs.

After practicing my two-step and flirting with some of the baddest bitches in the building on the dance floor, I headed to a room in the VIP section. The whole set-up looked real exotic with the red and black "freak me" theme. The lights were deeply dimmed and a bottle of Grey Goose vodka sat on the table chilling in a bowl of ice. I popped the top, then poured me a glass before sinking into the cushion of the giant chaise lounge. I was feeling good, I had money in my pocket, and I was starting to get a buzz from the Grey Goose. All I needed now was a freak bitch, and my evening would be complete. I smiled to myself and just as the thought of a naked woman popped in my head, two beautiful women walked through the door, explaining to me that they were lost. I invited them to come sit next to me, and then asked for their names and identification card before pouring them a glass of Goose, because they looked so young. To my surprise, they were legal and that's all I needed to know, because I definitely wasn't trying to be another R Kelly, Mike Tyson, or Mystikal. I pushed a button on the remote and watched as they gave each other a seductive look once they heard Keith Sweat's voice through the surround sound speakers. I poured a couple more glasses of Goose. They drank a couple more glasses, then one thing led to another, and before I knew it, we were French kissing while slowly undressing each other. In the nude, both girls looked as if God took his precious time, and sculpted every delicate curve on their bodies. Their breasts were a perfect C-cup, and had my mouth watering as they reminded me of four ripe cantaloupes, while the rest of their body captured my eyes daring me to look away. They both laid flat on their stomachs with their legs spread at an abnormal angle. I was kind of confused, because I had never witnessed anything like this, but they called it the paven, where two women laid on their stomachs side by side, and spread their legs until they reached the other's elbow, then slowly rotated their pelvises in a circular motion.

Damn. I was captivated, and wasted no time diving in, and taking turns blessing them both with my tongue that had the skills of a thirsty feline, licking, kissing and sucking their thick lips. I moved slowly to their puckered assholes, and licked their well-proportioned ass cheeks. I licked their tangy bitter assholes up and down, and then French kissed it to savor the taste. I then moved up and began rubbing my fingers back and forth over their clits with strong, quick movement at the same damn time. They sighed as I watched their eyes close, and their mouths fall open like oven doors. Their breathing increased and I accelerated the tempo of my fingers. I watched their puffy, swollen labia and then listened as they both came, moaning loudly and going stiff all over.

I grabbed the closest one, turned her over and rubbed my dick up against her pussy lips, before sinking in her. She placed her hands on my chest until I had my whole stick inside. Her pussy was so loose and sloppy, but I loved the way it felt. She moaned softly as I began slow stroking, then she pulled me closer to her and kissed me as I continued adjusting my speed. Her pussy walls clutched my dick and I swear, I thought I was gone cum everywhere.

By this time, her sister had recovered. She started to kiss her ass. I put more power in my thrusts, her big breasts shaking as the force of my fucking drove her into the cushion. When I leaned forward and sucked on a nipple, she moaned so I drilled her harder and harder. Her moans got louder and her pussy became sloppier. I put one hand beneath her to grab her ass, and worked a finger in her hole.

"Deeper...fuck me deeper! Yeah, oh yeah!" she cried as she got loose. My hips picked up the tempo and not too long after, she came like a flood in a city. Her whole body shook as pussy juices flooded her pussy and coated my dick. "Oh God, yes!" she went on moaning for what seemed like hours as tremors shook her body. I was still hard and began to work up on the tempo again, rotating my hips like I did on the dance floor. Soon she was going crazy again, yelling at the top of her lungs.

"Don't stop! Don't stop!" but she couldn't be selfish. I had plenty of dick to slang. I grabbed her and pulled her into a sitting position on top of me, with my dick still inside her, then laid back. Her sister got the hint, and came over to sit on my face, her tangy pussy was over my mouth, and her well- shaped ass cheeks draped over my nose. I started licking and slurping, and she started moaning and humping. The first one began humping me with all her power, and with every motion of her hips, I felt her pussy sliding up and down my pole. Her sister's pussy was so wet that her juices were flooding my mouth and nose. Although I couldn't see, I reached up, and grabbed her big breast. Now I had a mouthful of pussy, two handfuls of titties, and a model-type chick riding my dick like it was the last one in the world. I felt the throbbing in my dick and I guess she felt it too, because before I knew it, she had my dick in her mouth sucking me into a coma. I mean she slid up, swirling her tongue and cupping my balls, all at the same time. She slid up and down until I shot my load deep down her throat.

I woke up the next day feeling like a new man, and by the healthy bulge in front of my jeans, I could tell my lil' man was feeling good too. I crawled out of bed and did a couple push-ups and sit-ups. I knew I sent them two thots home last night satisfied, and feeling sorer than a quarterback who'd been sacked twenty times in one game. I put my dick game down something serious, and nobody in this world could tell me otherwise.

I walked into the bathroom to take a piss before brushing my teeth and washing my face. I was still feeling kind of sticky from last night, so I turned on the shower in attempt to take one, but my cell rang causing me to rush back to the room. The text message that had come through put a smile on my face.

"Hey baby, it's Ashlyn and Alice. We had a wonderful time last night, but I really wish we could've met in better circumstances, because we haven't had dick that good or a golden head in we don't know how long. Well, to get to the business of this text. My sister and I are HIV positive and have known for about three weeks now. And because you pissed off the wrong woman, welcome to the team. E'mani sent her love!"

I read the text over and over again, thinking this bitch had to be playing with me, because the way their pussy tasted, they couldn't have that shit. But then again, HIV doesn't have a taste, not that I knew of. I pushed speed dial to call and confront her about the message she sent, and my whole world turned upside down when the automated operator stated, "The person you are trying to reach has changed their number." They had me worried now. I ran back into the bathroom to turn the water off and dress, before grabbing my keys, and speeding out the door to my car. I knew the speed limit but didn't give a damn about it as I did almost seventy-five miles per hour, trying to get to the health department fast as I could. I was there for one reason and one reason only, and if the results were positive, I didn't know what I was gone do.

I jumped out of my car, walking straight up in the building like I owned the place. After two left turns, three right turns, and a walk down this long hallway, I broke down in tears. I turned to see Ashlyn and Alice's picture on the wall, amongst thousands of people who were HIV positive in St. Petersburg, Florida. I was literally on my hands and knees, crying like a hungry infant and lashing out at everybody who tried to be a good Samaritan by comforting me.

Ten minutes later, I was confronted by a doctor being curious to why I was crying in this specific part of the health department. "Son, don't take this the wrong way, because I really am trying to help, but have you had sexual relations with any of these people?"

I was shocked from him being so blunt, and anybody who looked could see the embarrassment on my face as I lied. "No sir, I just saw pictures of both of my little sisters, and I can't believe it." Once the words left my mouth, all he could see was my back because by that time, I was walking towards the door.

I sat in the car for a couple minutes before starting it and pulling off. It was only eleven thirty and I already felt like I'd had a long day, which was fucked up and I didn't think it could get any worse. Once I pulled up to my stash house to see what the count was for the week, I saw a red Ford Taurus zoom past like it was on a racetrack. I pushed it off as one of the young niggas in the hood stuntin', but I hadn't realized the mistake I made, until I saw a man in all-black stick an M-16 out the window and then the bright lights. "Who else wanna fuck with one of Hollywood hoes!" was all I heard as I choked on my own blood and felt my life slowly leaving my body.

Keith Williams

## Chapter Eleven
### E'mani

"Broadcasting live from around your way, I'm Brittany Collins, bringing you the latest of the latest. Around noon today, Jermaine 'Supreme' Waltson was found dead in the front yard of a suburban home owned by a Ms. Angel Gram, who turned out to be the girlfriend of Mr. Waltson. Upon investigation, it was said that a red Ford Taurus rode past, while an unknown passenger hung out of the window, firing a semi-automatic rifle until Mr. Waltson was no longer breathing. The car has not yet been found, and as of now, there are no suspects in custody. Stay tuned and we will update you with all new information as they come to us and remember, you heard it here first. I'm Brittany Collins, and this is Central Florida's trusted news station."

I stared at the TV as the news went off, while Nah Nah, Coco, Shanel, and Nicole stared at me. They knew who Supreme was and I would bet they were thinking the same thing I was thinking, they couldn't believe Supreme was actually dead. Now, I never told any of the girls that I sent Ashlyn and Alice at Supreme and that they both were HIV positive. I honestly regret doing so, because I believe in karma. What goes around comes around, so I really had to ask God for forgiveness and hope he forgives me. I never meant for them to kill him like that, because it can easily be traced back to them or even me, but then again, I don't even know if they were the ones who killed him or not.

"So, what now?" Coco asked, looking around at everybody. We were all in a daze and really didn't know what to do. I excused myself from everybody, walking straight to my room and the first thing I did was call Ashlyn. I needed some answers.

"I'm sorry, but the number you are trying to reach is no longer in service. Thank you. Goodbye," the operator stated, and the line went dead.

*Okay...I really wasn't expecting that*, I thought as I hung up my phone. Twenty minutes had passed before I realized I was looking like a statue staring at the wall. I was worried, but I wasn't worried. Whatever that meant. I just didn't think Ashlyn or Alice would drop a dime on me. Well, I was hoping they wouldn't. For the second time today, I really didn't know what to do. I knew I wasn't free from sin, and I definitely knew I was no Virgin Mary, but I had changed since I'd met Mahogany. It started with the way I dressed, the way I walked and sometimes, I even caught myself using slang, something I despise. Most of all, I would've never asked anybody to kill another person. My conscience was eating at me with so much pressure that I couldn't take it, and I broke down to my knees, praying like I never prayed before.

"Dear Heavenly Father, I come to you with a heavy heart, which has caused me to sin, and break one of your command-ments. Please give ear to my cries oh Lord, and forgive me, for I have trespassed against a precious child of yours." My face was soaked with tears as I talked to God and told him what was on my heart. "Pain and misery has surrounded me. You said ask and I shall receive, knock and the door shall be opened. Bring peace and comfort to my heart where I could forgive those who lie, cheat, steal, and swear against me, as well as forgive my sins, because I have come short of your glory. I truly believe in my heart that you sent your only begotten Son, so that whosoever believes in you shall not perish in hell but have everlasting life in Heaven. Father God, I am remorseful and once again, plead for your forgiveness. In Jesus name I pray. Amen."

I stayed on my knees and cried, thinking about how a man's life was cut short, because of me. I wasn't raised to hate, lie, or even murder, but somehow it was the words out of my mouth that dictated whether Supreme lived or died. It was time for me to confess my sin, and as embarrassed as I felt, I forced myself towards the door.

"If you're truly regretful and want forgiveness for your sins, please confess, and with the power of the Almighty God, your sins shall be forgiven, and with the strength of his forgiveness, shall you not perish in hell, but live an everlasting life through Jesus Christ," the voice echoed all around once I entered the booth of the confessional. I was so nervous, but I knew this was something

I had to do and I was really uncomfortable, but at the same time, the darkness gave me a sense of relaxation. Once I stopped shaking, I closed my eyes, and spoke as if I was talking to God again.

"I'm here to confess my sins and ask for mercy. I sent two of my friends out to kill an ex-boyfriend of mine. I knew they were HIV positive, but revenge got the best of me and today, the news revealed that he had been killed. What should I do, Father?"

"You have sinned beyond sins, and should be punished for your action, but God is a forgiving God and if you do everything I say of you, your sins shall be forgiven. First, I need for you to undress, remove every piece of clothing, including your panties," he responded.

My eyes shot open. I was confused by his request and as I stood there, he sensed my hesitation.

"Never doubt the Almighty God, for he gave you life, and he shall take it away. Your hesitation tells me your faith has been shattered, and you have not made reparation—"

"No, Father, please forgive me for I stand before you empty, humble and repentant, determined to amend my life, and resolved to make reparation, and do penance," I shouted, while stripping out of my clothes as if they were on fire. This was the first time I had ever been to a confessional, and I didn't want to make my situation worse by not doing what I was told. I listened, and waited on the father to respond or give me a sign of his dismissal, but all I heard was the muffled sound of two voices arguing back, and forward. One telling me to tweak my nipples, while the other voice shouted, "No, don't tell her that. I want to see her flick her clitoris."

I didn't know what to do. I was shocked, embarrassed, and confused all at the same time. I had never heard the father talk like that in the house of the Lord. Without hesitation, I dressed and got out of there fast as I could. I was contemplating on reporting them to the authorities but ignored the thought and went home. I had a feeling though that this experience was going to change me.

When I made it home, everybody was in the living room except for Mahogany. I tried to keep my feelings under control, but soon as I saw everybody staring at me, I broke down like a twenty-year-old Chevy. Nah Nah, Nicole, Shanel, and Coco all tried to comfort me like caring sisters, while Kayla sat on the couch and stared. I stared back at her, wondering where was the love, but got distracted by the girls drilling me with questions about what was wrong with me. I told them everything and even though these were my girls, I still felt embarrassed.

"See, that right there is why I don't go to church now. Even the pastors are hypocrites and horny ass perverts," Nah Nah stated.

"She's right, girl. I'm not saying stop believing in God, but you don't have to go to church to go to heaven. What if something bad would've happened to you?" Shanel joined in.

I was really thinking about taking their advice, and besides, I never liked going anyway, because I always had to sit next to the lady that couldn't make it to the restroom, and passed gas every five to ten minutes. It was Mama who forced me to go every Sunday, not caring if I wanted to or not. Right then and there, I made up my mind to never step foot in a church again, unless it was for a funeral or a wedding.

I glanced Kayla's way again, just to see if she was still there, because I hadn't heard her voice, and she gave me the nastiest look I had ever saw a person give. Everybody knew I wasn't a violent person, but I tooted my lips up and squinted my eyes, just to let her know I got the hint. There was bad blood between us, and I was about whatever she was about. She sucked her teeth and stormed out the door, slamming it hard as it closed. We all looked at each other confused, not knowing what had her panties in a bunch, but we brushed it off, assuming she was PMS-ing. Then again, she might still be upset about Mahogany and Nah Nah catching her on the couch doing the do with her lesbian lover. Personally, I didn't believe it when they told me. I just knew they were making everything up and trying to play jokes, but Kayla never denied the allegations and that told me everything. I couldn't imagine seeing her in the nude bumping her vulva with another woman, that's just nasty.

I had a hair appointment with my stylist scheduled for four o'clock at New Styles Salon, and it was already thirty-five minutes after three, so I excused myself and walked to my car after grabbing my purse.

It was so crowded when I got there that I was thinking about rescheduling, but my stylist, a handsome gay young man named Neeko, stopped me dead in my tracks by yelling my name across the room.

"Nice to see you again too, Neeko," I stated as I walked towards him, and pecked him on both cheeks. He then dismissed the woman who sat in his chair and patted the cushion, motioning me to sit down.

"What is going on with this on top of your head, honey?" he said in a feminine tone, while slightly pulling a tress of my hair. "Don't worry. That's what you hired me for. When I'm done with you, you're going to look like a bad bitch as always, but this time, I'm talking badder than Beyoncé and even Taraji Henson when she played Cookie on *Empire*."

I couldn't help but laugh, because even though he said it in a joking manner, he was serious as a heart attack. Out of the five women and two men who worked at New Styles Salon, I would bet Neeko had the most clientele. He just knew what we liked, and the craziest thing about him being a stylist at New Styles is that he's the only white person working in the whole shop. You could imagine all the haters he accumulates every day at the salon.

He finally finished washing and drying my hair, before trimming it the way I liked it. He was so slick with words that I let him talk me into dying burnt orange streaks into my hair. I hated to admit it, but the color really did look good on me, so I let him add the finishing touches by bringing out the hot curlers. He took his precious time, which I loved, and I was damn near knocked out when I saw somebody walking past wearing a black hoodie with Nah Nah's picture on the front, and the words "rest in peace" underneath it.

"What the..." I stated softly, doing a double take, and not be-lieving what I was seeing, but caught the back end of them as they walked out the salon. I spazzed out as I was now looking at a nude picture of Nah Nah, me, Mahogany, Coco, Shanel, Nicole, and Kayla together at our house on the side of the swimming pool.

"Sweetie, what is going on? Are you okay?" Neeko asked. My whole body felt paralyzed as fear took control of me. Only thing I could think about was getting home and warning the girls, but I couldn't move.

## Chapter Twelve
### Mahogany

"What the fuck is going on in here?" Nah Nah asked, looking from me to Kayla and then the other woman. I laughed, because I could see Kayla's lips forming the words it wasn't what it looked like, but she was cut short when her answer pissed Nah Nah off.

"You know the motto in this house. It's always what it looks like!" Nah Nah was right about that, and I couldn't refute it, because I was the one who came up with the rule, but I had to straighten my end and clear myself of this freak show Kayla was a part of.

"Hold up, Nah Nah," I said, trying to suppress the pain as I put my clothes back on. "Just to clear the smoke in the air, I don't do pussy. I'm a certified dick champion, so you can count me out of this equation and by the way, I just walked through the door not too long ago," I explained. Nah Nah knew how I rolled, and I would bet she had no doubt I was telling the truth.

Kayla, on the other hand, was caught red-handed. They literally still had their pussy lips connected, and looked as if they were striving for the longest kiss of Guinness World Records.

Most of us didn't have a problem with Kayla being gay, because she was our girl and we loved her but c'mon now, on the living room couch? That was so disrespectful.

Nah Nah was past the point of being furious. She wanted to beat Kayla's head in, because that lesbian shit didn't sit right with her, but I stopped it by jumping in between them. Kayla stared at the both of us for a long minute. When neither of us acknowledged her sincere look of apology, she and her bitch got dressed before disappearing out the front door.

I proceeded towards my room like a wounded animal but didn't make it, because I couldn't resist the need to soak in a tub full of hot water, so I made a detour to the bathroom.

When I stripped out of my clothes for the third time today, the light was shining directly on my body, giving me a more clear view as I looked in the mirror. Inspecting myself, I found blood mixed with blue lubricant in between my ass cheeks. It stung every time I touched it, and my blood boiled as I thought about Doe Boy violating my body. Tears instantly fell down my face and scenes from my past flashed before my eyes.

*"Mama, what's wrong with you?" I cried, shaking her uncon-scious body as she lay in bed staring at the ceiling like a zombie. I never could figure out why Mama was always in that state for hours at a time, but I knew it would happen every time I saw a needle, a burnt spoon, and white powder on top of her dresser.*

*After a while, I learned to just give her time and she would come back around, so I went to my room. I was developing pretty fast and becoming a young woman. I remembered Mama would always tell me once I was old enough and started growing hair on my private part, I should always keep it waxed, because men loved it that way. I really wasn't into boys at the time, but I could see strings of hair as I stared at my naked body in the mirror. I had been sneaking and stealing Mama's razors, waiting on this moment, and wanted to be prepared when it came. So like she taught me, I quickly sprinkled water between my spread legs, before lying on my bed, and carefully started shaving myself.*

*My cousin Shay, who had come home early from work, burst through my room door without knocking. I jumped from the shock of being surprised and tried to cover myself, but she had already caught me.*

*"Girl, what is you doing?"*

*"Nothing! Get outta my room!" I shouted as shame took over my face. My cousin Shay was a lesbian and was never the type to hide who she really was, no matter who liked it or not, so this was an awkward moment for me.*

*"You wanna be grown now. Well, I'm about to show you what grown women do," she shouted back, before rushing and pinning me to the bed. I kicked and screamed like my life depended on it, but no matter how much I squirmed like a fish out of water it was no use, because Shay outweighed me by at least thirty pounds. I fought until my voice was hoarse and my body went limp. I was*

*exhausted and thought Shay was too, before I felt her tongue between my legs and an electric shock shoot through my body.*

*Shay was sticking her tongue in and out of my coochie, while working her finger into my tight butt hole. The whole process felt weird, but I could feel myself getting moist from it as I moaned. "Yeah, that's it. Just relax, and let me taste this tight pussy," she moaned back.*

*I obeyed and relaxed like she said, hoping she would stop and leave me alone, but I got the surprise of my life when she stuck something huge, which I now know was a six-inch dildo inside of me, ripping my insides apart. I tried to scream, but nothing came out, while she forcefully pushed it in and out of me as blood soaked my bed sheets.*

I woke up from my daydream and wiped away my tears before stepping into the tub. The water turned red, but slightly eased the pain at the same time. I didn't know what I was gone do, but I knew one thing, Doe Boy was going to pay with his life. After about an hour, I was out the tub, dried myself off and then went to my room, and hit the bed laying flat on my stomach. The odd part about it was that I actually felt comfortable and was asleep like a hibernating animal in less than ten minutes.

It was about four o'clock in the afternoon when I woke up the next day. I couldn't believe I actually slept all day. I was usually the early bird, but I could tell my body needed the rest. I climbed out of bed, threw on a spaghetti strap dress, then flat ironed my hair before walking down the staircase. I heard the TV, but I didn't know if the girls were here or not. The closer I came to the end of the staircase, the more I realized why I only heard the TV

Nah Nah, Coco, Shanel, Nicole, Kayla, and E'mani were watching the news and I heard it with my own ears when they announced Supreme had been killed. The girls couldn't see me, because I was still halfway up the stairs, but close enough to where I could see the TV without being noticed. I felt my knees get weak and sat right there on the stairs before I had an accident. I couldn't believe Supreme was actually dead. I mean, I knew Doe Boy didn't play around about handling business, but Supreme was actually dead!

I hurried to my feet and ran back towards my room once I saw E'mani coming my way. I really didn't know why the hell I was running. Well, yes I did know. I didn't want the girls to think I was eavesdropping on them if they saw me just sitting on the stairs. Once E'mani walked out the door, I made my way back downstairs, and found myself the center of attention as Nah Nah, Coco, Shanel, and Nicole tried to tell me what happened to Supreme at the same time.

"Hold up! Hold up, I'm not deaf, and neither can I understand four people trying to talk to me at the same time, so all of y'all need to shut the fuck up!" I shouted over them. The whole room became quiet, and they stared at me like I was a circus act waiting to perform. When Nah Nah started to respond, she was quickly cut short by the news station, broadcasting Supreme's murder again. I watched, paying close attention for any sign of sloppiness because I couldn't afford an indictment. Knowing how muthafuckas snitching these days, I try to be extra careful.

They explained that Supreme had been gunned down in a drive-by, right outside Angel Gram's residence, his girlfriend. They then said that a neighbor, who wished to stay anonymous, provided them with a description of the suspects and also a license plate number. I stood there in shock as Hollywood's picture flashed over the TV screen as a person of interest. I had no idea Doe Boy even knew Hollywood, let alone used him as a hit man to kill Supreme. Shit, I could've done that my damn self. Knowing how pussy whipped I had Hollywood, he would've done anything I told him to do. I did my best to hide the fact that I knew Hollywood and act surprised by all this.

"Oh shit Mahogany, girl, ain't that's the dude we ran down on at Club Paid? The dude you tried to give a chance to get his red wings," Nah Nah asked in a half-serious, half-laughing manner.

"You right. That is him. How the hell his scary ass could be a person of interest? He couldn't even bust a grape in a fruit fight." We all burst into laughter because everybody knew how true that statement was. He showed us that at the club. I stood there a couple minutes contemplating my next move. I needed to take Doe Boy and Hollywood out of commission, at least before Hollywood had a chance to snitch and we all go down.

"I seriously need y'all help with something," I started before turning to look the girls in their eyes. I could see I had their full attention, and that made me feel more confident. "I know everybody here has each other's loyalty, but one thing you should always remember is, never let your loyalty to a person imprison you. I say that to say this, I don't want you to feel like you're obligated to do anything, just to show your loyalty to me. It's alright to say no and there wouldn't be no love lost."

All four girls looked at each other before turning their attention back to me and stood there. They let me know that they weren't going anywhere and that made me feel good, because I really was depending on them.

I broke everything down without leaving a single detail out. I told them about how I'd fucked Doe Boy to use him as ammunition to take Supreme out, and that I was also fucking Hollywood, the dude who actually killed Supreme, and whose picture had just flashed over the screen as a person of interest. I could tell they were all surprised by the look on their faces, but I explained that that wasn't the worse part. "Now, the last time I went to see Doe Boy, my plan was to fuck him, just to ease his mind before I dropped the bomb about handling Supreme, but somehow he thought just because of his boss status he could have what he wanted." I stopped to wipe the falling tears from my eyes, then took a deep breath before I continued. "That muthafucka violated by fucking me in my ass, and he got to pay with his life. That's why I need y'all help." I know they felt my pain, but I wanted them to really feel what I felt inside, yet they couldn't because they never experienced what I'd experienced.

Shanel tried to apologize to me, but I stopped her because I didn't need them to feel sorry for me. I needed their courage and willpower to help me get revenge. We all brainstormed before coming up with a foolproof plan and I had to admit I was amazed at all the evil thoughts we shared. "Double B's, bitch! Baller

Babies for life," Shanel shouted, and we all laughed like we had no worries, and wasn't just plotting to kill somebody. "We all should go get two big B's tattooed on our chest, right above our right breast. What y'all think?"

My loyalty was and always will be to my girls, and my girls were the Baller Babies, so I was down. Most of us agreed and for the ones who didn't, they did after a little convincing. So we mobbed to the car and once there, we texted E'mani to let her know the deal. We drove all the way to Orlando to a shop called Snapp Action Tattoos in Pine Hills, also known as Choppa City. By the name, you'd think they killed everything in sight, but once they saw five bad bitches hop out the car, they gave us a "G" pass.

"Cofio que rica estan estas, mami," was the greeting we received from a good looking brother who stood about six foot three, with broad shoulders and tattoos everywhere. I honestly didn't know what the hell he'd just said, but it sounded real disrespectful, and before I could open my mouth to respond, Nah Nah took the floor.

"Looking good is what we do best, papi." She then showed him a smile that could cause a roadblock. He stood there surprised, but what he didn't know was that Nah Nah is Dominican, and speaks Spanish fluently, so she knew exactly what he'd said.

"What that muthafucka said? 'Cause—"

"Fall back, Mahogany. He just said, 'Damn, these babies looking good.' That's it. He didn't say anything disrespectful," Nah Nah explained, after cutting me off in the middle of my sentence.

I fell back and relaxed like she said, until he finally told us his name and asked what we needed help with.

"We're all trying to get tatted up, and my brother Sweatt told me if I mention his name, you'll give us a deal, Tito, so what's up?" I asked.

"Sweatt? You talking 'bout Sweatt with two T's? Damn, that's my nigga. We did time together, and I did damn near his whole body. You said you his sister? I got y'all," he said excitedly before escorting us to the back of the shop.

I laid on the couch and went under the gun first and honestly, I was ready to cry because I had never gotten a tattoo, but it didn't hurt at all. I took it like a gangsta.

## Chapter Thirteen
### E'mani

I tried to lift my arms and legs, but realized they had been strapped to the salon chair. Neeko and I were the only ones there, so when I yelled for help, my cries fell on deaf ears. I couldn't understand why he would do something like this to me. I thought we were friends, but I didn't realize how naive I was until he slapped me across the face, drawing blood from my lip.

"Why are you doing this to me, Neeko? I know this isn't you—"

"Shut the fuck up! You think you know me, but you really don't know anything about me. This sissy ass job at the salon isn't me. I'm a professional hit man, and you've been on my list for a while now. With my boss PMS-ing all the time and having bitch fits, she didn't know what she wanted to do, so she made me wait," Neeko cut me off, angry that I was talking too much.

Despite the situation I was in, I couldn't stop myself from laughing in his face. I just couldn't see Neeko being a hit man. He was too damn feminine for one, and two, he was a hundred pounds soaking wet. He once again slapped me across the face, erasing the smile from my lips, as he gave me a wicked grin. I cried from the shock of not expecting it, more than the pain the slap actually caused. I couldn't remember ever being hit so hard that my tears didn't fall as I cried out.

"Help me!" I struggled and yelled until my body felt sore. I was trying to get the attention of a bystander or anybody that could help." I've been kidnapped."

He quickly covered my mouth with his hands to muffle the sound of my voice, then slapped me repeatedly, sending me into a daze. The pain was unbearable and I could feel my face swell as I knew a black eye was next to come. I went in and out of consciousness, praying it wasn't my time to meet my maker.

He shouted at me and I could see his lips moving, but couldn't understand a word that came out. I felt worse than I did the night Mahogany caught me and Supreme together and I got drunk for the first time. I hated it. Neeko started towards me until we were face-to-face. For a minute, I thought he was going to kiss me on the lips, but what he did next was the last thing I would've thought him to do, which was untie my hands and feet.

"Some people want it all, but I don't want nothing at all if it ain't you, baby. If I ain't got you, baby." My cell phone started ringing, catching the both of us by surprise, and that was all it took. I was so determined to escape that when the first chance presented itself, I was outta there.

While Neeko was standing there trying to locate my ringing phone, I sprinted full speed towards the salon door, like the typical white girl in a horror movie. Soon as I got to the door, I met the floor face-first, tripping over my own legs. Our introduction didn't last that long though, because just as quick as I fell, I was back on my feet with Neeko now right on my heels.

"Help me, please," I yelled as I ran like Forest Gump. I yelled and continued running, bypassing the women with their kids while they stared at me. I didn't care. I was so scared I didn't realize how far I had run until I was a block away from my own house. "Please be home. Please be home," I chanted, hoping the girls would be in the house to comfort me when I made it there. The closer I got, the more tears slid down my face. I know I was acting real hysterical, but I didn't give a damn at the moment. I needed some love and support.

"Mahogany, Nah Nah, Nicole, Coco, Shanel," I yelled, soon as I stepped into the house. I looked in every room, high and low, before shouting their names again and still got no response. I felt more alone than I'd ever felt in my life.

It was like the walls were closing in on me as so much pressure built up, causing me to lose consciousness and I hit the floor with a loud bang at the same time my window shattered into thousands of pieces.

I woke up almost twenty-eight hours later with tubes everywhere, through my nose, mouth, and arms as the realization hit me that I was in a hospital. My tongue felt like sandpaper. The sky was pitch-black and once again, I was alone. I cried to myself, feeling sorry. I cried for my family and friends not being here when I needed them the most, and I cried from the pain that shot through my right shoulder every time I moved. I wanted to scream so bad, but the tube traveling down my esophagus took my voice away. The first thing that popped in my head was to pray, but my heart was now so full of hatred that I didn't know who God was anymore. I wanted to say fuck him so many times for taking me through so much pain, my head started pounding.

"OmiGod, baby, you're awake. Thank God," I heard a familiar voice say. I looked to my left where it came from, and I swear I felt like a child who had just reunited with her family when I saw my mother's face. I smiled, then tried to speak, but she stopped me by putting her fingers to my lips. "Shhhhh...honey, don't talk. Save your energy." I wanted to protest, but decided not to because I did actually feel weak. She noticed I was crying and wiped the tears from my face. "It's all going to be okay, honey. I'm here," she stated then hugged me, pulling my head to her chest. I wanted to believe her, but I knew I couldn't because she didn't understand what was really going on, or that somebody was trying to kill me and my girls. She did tell me I had been shot though, and how I ended up in a hospital bed. Despite everything that happened, I wanted to cry tears of joy when she told me that Mahogany, Nicole, Nah Nah, Coco, and Shanel had been here the whole time I was unconscious, but left not too long ago to freshen up. My girls had been here for me all along, I thought.

My mother stayed by my side until I was discharged, which was when the sun rose, and my doctor came to sign the papers. My injury wasn't life threatening, but the doctor did say I needed to get some rest, and being the caring person my mother was, she drove me straight to her house where I was forced to stay until she felt like I was well enough to take care of myself.

I grabbed the cordless phone to call Mahogany. I wanted to let her and the girls know that I was okay. I also needed to give them a heads up about Neeko and the person who had the hoodie on with our picture on it, but to do so I had to keep an eye out for my mother, because I knew she was an eavesdropper.

"Hello?" Mahogany answered on the second ring.

"Mahogany, this is E'mani. How you doing?"

"OmiGod, E'mani, you woke up. I was thinking the worst, and we all were ready to go shoot somebody shit up to feel our pain. Who shot you?" she asked, taking off and thinking about herself as usual by not giving me a chance to finish my sentence. I let it ride, because I didn't want to start an argument, and I knew this was her way of showing she was worried about me.

"Listen Mahogany," I started. "Somebody is trying to kill us, and it's not Supreme. While I was at the salon, I saw somebody wearing a black hoodie that had a picture of Nah Nah on the front with the words 'rest in peace' at the bottom, and then on the back, there was a picture of all of us. Me, you, Nah Nah, Nicole, Coco, Shanel, and Kayla were skinny dipping in the pool, which is supposed to be personal. The question I want to know is, how did they get that?" I stopped for a minute to catch my breath. I definitely didn't want to relive the horror I went through at the salon with Neeko, but I had to tell her.

"I don't know who was wearing the hoodie, but I do know my stylist Neeko is working with them. He kidnapped me and tried to kill me, but I got away. He was the person that shot me"

She explained to me that she didn't know what was going on, and didn't know who was trying to kill us, but suggested I stay with my mother until they could figure something out. I wasn't feeling that at all. I knew I wasn't much of a fighter, but I wasn't useless. We talked a little while longer before I hung up, and shifted my thoughts to the situation at hand. Who would be trying to kill us? I thought real hard about it, almost catching a headache in the process.

I didn't know if it was somebody I knew or what, but all Neeko talked about was how his boss was PMS-ing and having bitch fits, so I knew she was a female. I walked to my old room to see if Mama had changed anything since I'd moved out, and it surprised me that it was exactly the way I'd left it. All my stuffed animals crowded the bed and the picture of Daryl Nicks, my first love, was resting on my headboard. I don't know why, but that picture made me think about Supreme and how good it felt when he would make love to me. I mean, really make love to me, not just fuck me. I was thinking about the time Supreme pissed me off, and I wouldn't let him fuck me for a whole week. All I let him do was eat my pussy. He ate it so sloppy that I came so hard and left a wet spot on my bed for two days from my orgasm. I smiled to myself because I was starting to get wet. I hadn't had sex since Supreme, and I was so backed up and frustrated I believed if I did, I would probably ejaculate like a man.

My mother walked in on me staring at Daryl's picture and without asking, I knew she was thinking the opposite of what I was really feeling. "You miss him, don't you?" she asked. I knew Mama liked Daryl and thought he was Mr. Right for me, but she didn't really know Daryl. She only saw what he wanted her to see of him. She used to always ask why I broke his heart by leaving him and getting with a thug, but what Mama didn't know was that it was Daryl who broke my heart, by dumping me when I told him I missed my period and might be pregnant.

"No, Mama. I don't miss him. He's a jerk and I don't know why you still have this picture in this house." I took the picture out the frame, then tore it into tiny pieces before throwing it into the trashcan where it belongs. I could tell Mama didn't like it, but what could she really say. It was my picture and I could do whatever I wanted with it. She walked away without saying a word and I shrugged my shoulders, because the day was already turning sour.

I laid down on my bed careful not to bump my arm, which was hanging in a sling from my gunshot wound. I couldn't do anything, but think or maybe read a book. I hated feeling so vulnerable, and I felt like that every time I was back at my mother's house.

### Chapter Fourteen
**Mahogany**

Nah Nah was last to get tatted and for some reason, she wanted to talk to Tito alone, while the rest of us waited for her in the front of the shop, with some freaked out ass white dude that had tattoos all over his face. We talked a little shit, but we let her handle her business, whatever it was. We didn't cock block on a bitch, that wasn't our style.

We admired each other's tats while we waited, even though we all had the two big B's we had different styles. Some of us had more details than others. Mine was the cutest though if anybody asked me, and nobody had to tell me because I knew I was the shit with my new tat. On the other hand, we all felt like we were the baddest bitch, and honestly, Trina needed to sit her washed-up ass down.

Nah Nah finally walked through the door after about twenty minutes and the whole world could tell she'd been doing the nasty. She had the just-fucked hairstyle going, and was rocking it like it was the newest fashion. I didn't say a word as we walked to the car, but that didn't mean I didn't want to know every detail. I just didn't want to embarrass her by asking in front of strangers, so I waited until we were all alone.

"What happened back there, girl? And I want to know every single detail," I asked, soon as we got to the car and away from outsiders.

"Hold up. Can we get in the car first with your nosey ass?" she shot back. We all slightly laughed, but I knew they wanted to know just as bad as I did. We jumped in the car at the same time with Shanel behind the wheel, and we weren't even a block away before I asked again.

"What's up? I don't like that you got a bitch waiting, let us know what happened."

She smiled a big ass Kool-Aid smile like a shy schoolgirl, before taking the floor. "First, yeah, his dick was big and no, he is not a golden head, because I know one of you was gone ask that.

But this nigga was on some porn star style shit. He had me in so many crazy positions that I literally felt like a pretzel. A horny ass pretzel. He fucked me on the couch, the table, the floor, the wall, and then he picked up my lil' ass, and walked around while I bounced on that dick, bounced-bounced on that dick."

The whole car burst out laughing as Nah Nah did her freak dance and showed us her love faces.

"You nasty, freak-ass bitch. Now people gotta get their tattoo on that same table and couch you just fucked on. I'm glad I already got mine," Nicole stated.

"I hope you don't think I'm the first bitch he fucked like that, because if you is, you gotta be trippin'. I can tell you right now that nine times out of ten, you already laid all over his kids and another bitch's pussy juices," Nah Nah shot back.

Now that comment had all of us feeling like we had the cooties, because we were just on those same spots not too long ago. We continued to talk shit to each other while we drove home. I know if we were around anybody else, they would've been quick to judge Nah Nah by saying she was a thot for doing what she did, but we didn't because she was our girl and anyone of us would've did the same thing if we felt how she felt.

We made it home in about an hour to find police everywhere. I swear I thought somebody had got killed in our house. Shanel parked and all of us ran past the police and to the front door without saying a word to anybody.

"Can I help you ladies?" one of the officers at the door asked, while blocking us from going inside.

"Get your fuckin' hands off me. This is our damn house." It seemed as though we all said the same thing at the same time. He still didn't let us in, so like the ghetto bitches people think we are, we all called him everything but the child of God, until we witnessed them bringing E'mani's unconscious body out on a gurney and blood everywhere.

"Omifuckin' God..."

"Somebody tell me what the fuck happened..."

"E'mani, get up..."

I heard screaming coming from every direction as I cried for the family of the person who was responsible for this, because believe me, they were about to start picking out their black dresses. I ran, and jumped in the ambulance after telling the girls to follow in the car. The paramedics kept telling us that she was alive when I asked, but I swear I couldn't see her chest moving. I looked out the window the whole ride to the hospital, because I couldn't stand seeing her like that. Once there, we all had to wait in the lobby while they did an emergency surgery, and I took that opportunity to call Mrs. Newman and give her all the details of what I knew, which wasn't much at all.

She showed up about forty-five minutes later, looking her age. I could tell she was stressed out, and the wrinkles on her face told the story of the struggle and hard times she'd been through in her life. I gave her a hug and introduced everybody before sitting back down and continued waiting. We didn't know how E'mani was progressing, and by the look on everybody's faces, that had us worried. I'm talking about to the point where I wanted to go paint the city red, to get my mind off her.

After about two hours, the doctor finally let us in the back to see her, and the sight of her being connected to so many tubes broke me down. I cried like I'd never cried before. Seconds turned into minutes, and minutes turned into hours. Mrs. Newman was acting so strong that I admired her strength and allowed her to comfort me. She told me to stop crying because God had plans for E'mani. We just had to leave it in his hands, and let him work. I really wasn't a religious person, so all that talk about God went in one ear and out the other. We stayed there for two whole days, waiting for E'mani to open her eyes and nothing happened. I was contemplating my next move because I really wanted to go home and take a shower, but I didn't want to leave and E'mani wakes up.

"I can see it in your eyes that you ladies are tired. Go home, take a shower, and get yourselves some rest," Mrs. Newman said out of the blue, like she was reading my mind. I tried to convince her that we were alright, but she wouldn't take no for an answer, so after promising we'd be back in a couple hours, we left.

It wasn't long before we made it to the house and found it still looking like a crime scene. There were bloodstains left on the carpet and glass everywhere from the shattered front window. We all cleaned up together before retiring to our rooms and taking turns in the shower. I never knew how hard it was to get blood out of a carpet until today. I finally got to sleep after thirty minutes of laying in my bed, staring at the ceiling, and my cellphone started ringing a tone that sounded like a marching band in my ear. It rang so loud and for so long that I wanted to break it when I reached for it, but somehow, I ended up hitting the wrong button and a familiar voice came on the line. I couldn't believe it when E'mani said her name. I swear I thought I was dreaming, until I heard the worry in the tone of her voice.

She went on to explain something about her stylist kidnapping her, somebody was wearing a hoodie with our picture on it, and that somebody was trying to kill us. She had just dropped an atomic bomb on me with all this information. I already had enough on my plate, and now she just added another full course meal. I suggested that she continue to stay with her mother for a while, and then we hung up. I didn't really know what I was going to do about this new situation, but I had to deal with them one at a time, and I chose Doe Boy as my first choice.

The next day couldn't have come fast enough for me. It was about eight o'clock in the morning when we got on the road headed to Atlanta. Nicole drove while I rode in the passenger seat, and Nah Nah, Coco, and Shanel sat in the back. We sat in silence as we rode, mentally going over our plan. Doe Boy had been hearing about this clique of women on the rise, who called themselves the Baller Babies. He heard about the stunts we pulled when we balled out at Club Paid. Every chance he got, he told me something he'd heard about us, like he was really praising the ground we walked on. I knew it would come as a surprise when I told him that I was the head of the Baller Babies, and I could set up a meeting for him to meet the girls if he wanted. The first phase of executing my plan was to make him feel comfortable, so being that we were his guests, and he felt like he had me under his control, his ego was as big as a house.

We sashayed through the double doors of Magic City without being searched. I scanned the room and located four bouncers, without a problem. It was daylight outside and the club was closed, so it wasn't any use for more to be there. They all stood not too far from the entrance, so I knew Doe Boy had told them about us, which was the reason they stood there looking like horny ass dogs.

"Mahogany, baby, you look beautiful," Doe Boy said as he embraced me in a hug. I hugged him back, smiled then introduced the girls.

"Doe Boy, this is Nah Nah, Nicole, Coco and Shanel, and yes, they are twins so don't ask. Girls, this is the boss man, Doe Boy," I shot back. He shook all their hands before offering us a drink of tequila. He knew that was my favorite so I took mine to the head and watched as the girls did the same. I was already feeling like too much time was being wasted, so I winked at Nah Nah to get her on point, then walked up to Doe Boy and grabbed a handful of his dick while licking his ear.

"Would you ladies mind showing these gentlemen a good time while I take care of my business?" I suggested out loud before walking Doe Boy to his office with his hand searching under my skirt.

He started ripping off his clothes like they were on fire, soon as the door closed, and I smiled slowly easing my .45 out of my boot. I figured once he got down to his boxers, he'd look up, wonder why I was still dressed and that's exactly what he did. "Baby, what are you doing?" he asked, stumbling over his words. "You robbing me now?"

I walked closer to where he was and slapped him with the butt of my gun, watching as he fell to the ground holding his face as blood poured from his nose. "You knew this shit wasn't going to last forever. When you do the things you do and treat people the way you treat them, it comes back on you. always remember that. Now where is the money?"

He cried like a baby, not because I was robbing him, but because he said he thought we had something special between us. He followed my instructions though, and filled four bags with money once he stood to his feet. I knew this wasn't even half of what he had, but I didn't care. I just wanted to get this over with. "Bitch, you think you gone make it out of here alive. I'm Doe Boy. I'll have every muthafucka you know tryna kill you, so I hope it was worth it," he shouted, now growing some nuts. I adored the way he turned up like a car stereo, and even the killer mug he put on as we walked out of his office, but I got the last laugh when he viewed all four of his bouncers laid flat on the floor, naked with guns to their heads.

"What happened to all that big boy talk? The cat got yo' tongue now?" I asked, watching as he scanned the whole room, mouth wide open. I loved the look he had on his face to be honest, I think my pussy got wet when I viewed it, but I needed to laugh a little more. "Take your dick out and hold it in your hand," I demanded. Doe Boy, along with everybody else looked at me like I was crazy, but I wasn't, and I meant what I said. I let off a shot by his ear, hoping to burst his eardrum for hesitating. "You think I'm playing with you?"

Without a second thought, he held his uncircumcised dick out to me. I tried to hold back my laughter, but the sight of it shriveled up had me cracking up. I could tell he was embarrassed, but he was about to die anyway, so it really didn't matter. After I calmed down and focused, I made him pull the foreskin back to reveal the head then pointed my gun direct at it, and pulled the trigger. Blood splattered all over me as the whole ATL heard Doe Boy scream and fall to the ground, holding his dick where the head used to be. I turned to view everybody's reaction, and I was the only one getting a thrill out of what I was seeing.

"Mahogany. Stop playing around, and shut that nigga ass up," Nah Nah shouted over Doe Boy yelling. She was right. I was doing a little too much, and he was starting to give me a headache so without warning, I sent a hollow point straight through the back of his head. Soon as his body went still, the Baller Babies cleaned house, leaving no witnesses alive.

"For those of you who even let the thought cross your mind that you can fuck with the Baller Babies, you might want to go kill yourself before we do. Double B's, bitch!" I shouted, staring straight into the camera.

Keith Williams

## Chapter Fifteen
### E'mani

Sleep didn't come easy for me the last couple nights. I tossed, and turned, because my shoulder was killing me, and Mama kept her gospel music playing until three o'clock in the morning. I mean, I love the voices of some of the gospel singers, but damn, Mama, what the fuck? I really wanted to say something, but I didn't. Honestly, what could I say? She was my mother, and this is her house I'm staying in.

I mumbled a couple words under my breath, happy she wasn't around, and then caught myself putting my hand over my mouth. I don't know what had gotten into me, but I'd been using profanity a lot lately. It had to come from being around the girls. They use it like it's the only language they know.

I don't know why but all of a sudden, the image of Kayla popped in my mind, the scene of her and another woman eating each other's pussies. That is so fuckin' gross, knowing they both bleed faithfully every month. That's just nasty. I wonder if she was alright though, because nobody had seen her since that day we found out Supreme was killed, and the day I went to the salon.

*OmiGod*! I thought. Could Kayla be the person I saw with the hoodie on? She'd been missing in action. She was one of the few people who knew I was at the salon, and that would explain the nude picture of us. I didn't think Kayla would've went that far as to try and get me killed, but then again, I didn't know her like I thought I did. I had a little more investigating to do before I told Mahogany or even accused Kayla of something she might not have had anything to do with. But something deep down in the pit of my stomach was telling me she's in the midst of everything, and I believed it.

"E'mani, you up?" my mother asked from the hallway en route to my room. "I know you're not well right now, but my rules haven't changed. No sleeping in. So you need to find something to do."

*She couldn't be serious,* I thought. I mean, look at me. Did she forget that I was practically handicapped? What the hell could I do? I laid there, and just stared at her while she stared back. I didn't have any intentions of moving, but if she continued to try and make me do what she wanted because this was her house, I was outta here.

"E'mani, did you hear what I said?"

"I'm outta here. I don't have to deal with this shit," I snapped, getting out the bed.

The look on my mother's face said a thousand words as she stared at me, looking like she was about to have a seizure.

"Excuse me? E'mani Shanel Newman, I know you didn't just use profanity in my house. "Girl, are you out of your mind? And don't you keep walking when I'm talking to you."

I walked through the threshold of the door without looking back. Shanel had went and got my car from the salon where I'd left it, but I still had to catch the bus, because she drove it home instead of to me. It was a good thing I'd kept a little extra money in my pockets to get around, because I didn't have a phone or purse. I caught the Metro bus to the Greyhound station, then from the Greyhound station to St. Pete. People were looking at me crazy, but I didn't care. I sat all the way in the back so I was somewhat alone to give myself a chance to meditate.

Everything was going smooth until I stepped off the bus in St. Pete, where the K-9 unit was running around searching for drugs. I walked past the baggage claim, and that's when it happened. The K-9 dog ran right up to me and stuck its head underneath my dress, making it flair up. I tried to push it away gently as I could, but it growled at me before opening its mouth to bark. I stood there frozen, afraid it might bite me while bystanders watched like I was on a TV show.

"Ma'am, do you have illegal drugs on your person?" asked the first officer who walked up to me.

"Drugs!" I shouted, embarrassed he was causing a scene in front of so many people.

"Yes, ma'am. Drugs. My dog smells something under your dress. He's trained to bark, and then sit when he's found something, so ma'am, would you mind coming with us for a strip search?"

I couldn't believe this shit was happening to me. It was like I was having so much bad luck. They took me to a small room where I was told to wait until they contacted a female officer. I was freezing my ass off for what felt like an hour when two female officers walked in and introduced themselves as Officer Rose and Officer Walker

"Would you mind taking off your sling first? And if you need a hand, I don't mind helping you," Officer Walker asked. It kind of surprised me that they were calm, and talked to me with respect, and not like a convict. That made me relax a little, and comply with their demands. I was then told to remove my dress, bra, and panties before squatting down and coughing. I felt humiliated once I did that, because on top of me stripping in front of two women, my nipples were starting to get erect from them coming into contract with the cool air.

Once the two officers didn't find anything out of the ordinary, they apologized for the inconvenience, then offered to drive me home. I accepted their offer, because I really was too embarrassed to be around the people at the Greyhound station after everything that had just happened. We rode the whole way in silence, which I appreciated, because I wasn't trying to get familiar with the police.

"Mahogany, Nah Nah, Nicole, Coco, Shanel," I shouted their names once I walked through the door. At first, I was starting to get worried because it was like déjà vu, but then a minute later, they all came running to where I was standing.

"OmiGod, E'mani! Girl, you look a hot mess. How did you get here?" Nicole asked. I felt like a hot mess after all I had just gone through, and having a casual conversation was not something I wanted to do at the moment.

"It's a long story, and right now, I don't feel like talking about it," I explained, then walked to my room, simple and fast. I knew once again that they were just worried about me, but I didn't mean no harm. I just wanted to be alone. From all the events that took place today, and the restless nights I experienced at my mother's house, I was exhausted and think I fell asleep soon as I found a comfortable spot on my bed. My body needed it bad, and I was surprised it hadn't shut down on me before now.

I slept like Snow White, as two days passed before I awoke from my hibernation. I woke up well rested and everything. My body felt energized, my shoulders felt like they were good enough for me to play in the NFL with the fellas, and I felt like I could run a marathon at this very moment. Yes, I felt good. I jumped in the shower for about thirty minutes, then brushed my teeth before getting dressed and walking downstairs.

"Damn, Sleeping Beauty. About time you woke yo' ass up. I thought you was dead up there for a minute," Shanel said, before laughing. Everybody was on the couch watching *106 and Park Top 10 Countdown* on BET, except for Kayla, who was still MIA. I didn't say anything about it, because I didn't want anybody to feel some type of way, but if anybody asked me, I still felt like she had something to do with me getting shot.

They all made room for me on the couch as we watched Chris Brown dance, while fantasizing about him throwing that dick on us like he was doing the girl on TV as they completed their routine. I never thought about what I would do if I ever met Chris Brown, until now. The way he moved his body like a snake ready to attack, I know he'd bang this pussy if I bust it open in front of him. I looked around to see if anybody was watching, then blushed from embarrassment when I caught Coco staring at me, and laughing when she caught me.

"E'mani, you alright? You over there making love faces and smiling to yourself. You know we can get you some help if you need it."

Everybody turned to look at me at that point, but it was too late, wasn't anything to see except for my pearly white teeth. I rolled my eyes at her for trying to be funny, and almost broke my neck doing a double take at the new tattoo they all had on their chests.

"What is that?" I asked, trying to get a better view as they shielded theirs from my vision.

"It was supposed to be a surprise. When I count to three, we gone move our hands," Coco stated, then counted. When she got to three, they removed their hands. I had to admit that I was jealous, and wanted to wring their necks for going to get a tattoo without me, knowing I wanted one too.

"That's how you all do me? Go and get tattoos and not take me?" I asked, mean mugging everybody.

"I did text you and let you know, but I guess you were too busy getting kidnapped to read it," Mahogany finally opened her big mouth, taking my kidnapping as a joke. I really wanted to wring her neck now, my situation was serious and I didn't see anything funny about it.

I got closer to their chests, inspecting every detail each of them had, and I could feel myself starting to hate. I just couldn't get over the fact that they got tatted up without me, so to feed my satisfaction, I ran by and slapped every last one of them in the chest, watching as they almost jumped out of their panties from the pain.

"Ohhh...bitch, I'ma kill you."

"You better hope you didn't scratch my tattoo."

"Don't worry, that ass is mine when I catch you."

"I'm right behind her, so it's gone be a double ass whoopin'. Believe that," they all shouted after each other. I wasn't worried though, because as long as I had this sling over my shoulder, they wouldn't lay a finger on me with too much pressure.

They stood there in their feelings like I had just called them out of their names, and I knew they wanted to kill me, by burying me alive right now. I just laughed because we all loved each other, and there was nothing in the world we wouldn't do to help each other, and I do mean nothing.

## Chapter Sixteen
### Mahogany

Before we left Magic City, I grabbed the DVD that showed the security video, and then we set the building on fire. Burn baby, burn.

While the drive back to Florida was all but boring, I was surprised we didn't get pulled over for being so wild. We were turned all the way up. I'm talking about CD player booming, Nicole driving eighty miles per hour, and Nah Nah throwing money all over the car. We were straight up trippin', but we made it home safe, thank God.

Once there, we counted the four bags of money and I damn near cried, because the half a mil couldn't have come at a better time. Yeah, I said it right, a half damn mil, and that wasn't even a quarter of what Doe Boy was working with, that I knew of, because there had been times where I sat and watched Doe Boy put five and six million in three or four different money machine counters, or whatever you call them things that count your money for you.

We all split the money equally, which meant everybody received a hundred thousand dollars apiece, before calling it a night. When I woke up the next morning, I brushed my teeth, and got myself together before waking the whole house up. I went to each room in the house and, if there was somebody in it, then it was time to raise them from the dead.

"Top of the morning, sleepy heads," I said, then pulled the comforter from over them.

"Mahogany! OmiGod, I'ma kill you," most of them yelled, because they were sleeping naked. I laughed, because it wasn't like I'd never seen pussy before. Shit, I got one myself. They just better be glad I didn't wake their asses up with a pot full of ice cold water.

"We're about to go to a very important meeting, so you all have ten minutes to get fly or I'm leaving without you. and I'm not playing," I shouted. then waited.

Ten minutes turned into thirty, because everybody had to take a shower, do their hair, and then find something to wear. After seeing everybody in the living room, it was well worth the wait. We looked just like movie stars, bad bitches and divas.

We jumped in E'mani's Magnum, because it was the only one of our cars that had enough room for all five of us to ride comfortably. I still hadn't told them where we were going and for that, they were damn near about to jump me.

"Alright, alright!" I shouted over all the screaming and yelling. "Can you all keep a secret?"

They looked at me like I was stupid and then somebody stated. "Now you know we can keep a secret."

"Well, so can I, so stop asking because I'm not telling, " I shot back and then laughed. They mugged me, not liking that the joke was on them.

We cruised for about two hours, until I pulled up in front of a ten-foot gate, which surrounded a house I guessed cost over a million dollars.

"Where are we?" asked Nah Nah.

"We're in Palm Beach, where the real killas roam. So, you might want to hide all yo' shit," Nicole answered for me.

I was kind of shocked and wondered how she knew we were in Palm Beach. but then it hit me. This was where she was raised. and hustled almost all her life.

"This shit weak," Nah Nah replied, looking around.

"This ain't got nothing on Brooklyn, New York. My niggas will come down here and murda all these pussies. Straight up."

I laughed at the facial expression Nicole gave Nah Nah, because I knew she felt some type of way. Even though I was laughing, I felt like they were arguing over something stupid. I mean. neither of them owned Brooklyn, New York or Palm Beach, Florida,

After a while, I got out of the car, followed by Coco and Shanel. Once Nah Nah and Nicole realized we weren't paying them any attention, they jumped out to catch up.

"You are such beautiful women and it is an honor to finally meet all of the ladies behind the name Baller Babies. I've been hearing nothing but good things about you all. Welcome to my home," Mr. Montoya greeted us.

Once again, I was staring at the connect's connect. I mean, the real brick mason. He got his coke straight off the leaf. I didn't really know that much about him. but the first time Doe Boy brought me to meet him, he'd told me his family owned the land that grew the coca leaf and produced the coke.

Anyway, Mr. Montoya was full-blooded Cuban and always spoke like he owned the world. He stood about five foot ten, with a slim frame and weighed no more than a hundred and seventy-five pounds, with hands that could cover my whole face.

He invited us in and ordered his butler to fix us some drinks, before escorting us to his sitting room. Everything I laid my eyes on looked expensive, from the cigar he puffed to the wine glasses.

"I just received the word of Doe Boy's death and I would like to know if you know anything?" Mr. Montoya asked. Now, I could have risked all our lives and told Mr. Montoya that we killed Doe Boy, without knowing what his intention was, but that would be dumb and I'm far from that, so I straight up lied.

"OmiGod! When did this happen? I had no idea he was dead."

All four of my girls looked at me like I was crazy, trying to catch on to what I was doing.

"Yeah, somebody killed him. It don't matter though. I called you here to see if you wanted to take his place. I know this is a man's world, but with everything I've heard about the Baller Babies, I know you all can handle it," Mr. Montoya shot back. All of us knew he was trying to give us a chance of a lifetime. I mean, we could be bigger than the black widow, Nicki Bums, the Cocaine Cowboys and even Pablo Escobar, but more money meant more problems and that we weren't trying to go through.

"Thank you, Mr. Montoya, but no thanks. That's just something we're not ready for, the amount of cocaine you were giving Doe Boy is out of our league, and the consequences that come with us making mistakes outweigh the money we could make and for the record, I'm not talking about the consequences from the authorities."

After a little more explaining, he understood where I was coming from, but I felt I owed it to him to find somebody who was good for the job and in my mind, there was nobody more eligible than my brother, Sweatt. He started asking so many questions when I mentioned Sweatt's name. He wanted to know his whole life story, but I couldn't blame him. Even though my face was good, he didn't know my brother, and he didn't want to slip by doing business with somebody he didn't know. I told him everything he needed to know, then we agreed that I could give Sweatt his number, so they could talk and get to know each other before they met and did business. I knew beyond a reasonable doubt that Sweatt was loyal and about his business, but that wasn't going to stop me from jumping in his chest about ever crossing Mr. Montoya, because I was putting my face on him.

We hung out for about another hour and then jumped back on the interstate. This time, Shanel drove while I sat in the back behind the driver's seat. I had a lot on my mind at the time and my head felt like I had been hit with a Cîroc bottle. I didn't know what was going on with Kayla, if she was safe or if she was even alive. She left a couple days ago and we hadn't seen or heard from her since. She wasn't answering her cell phone and yesterday, I'd found out that she had changed her number. Something just didn't feel right, but I always know what was done in the dark will eventually come to light.

We made it home in no time. Actually, it seemed we made it back faster than we made it there. We changed clothes, then met back in the kitchen. At the same time, while we waited on the oven to heat up, we went to talking about life in general until we heard somebody yelling our names like they were crazy. We ran to the living room, not believing somebody just walked into our house.

"OmiGod, E'mani! Girl, you look a hot mess. How did you get here?" Nicole asked. We all were happy to see her, but I guess she didn't feel the same, because soon as she said what she said, she walked off to her room. We let her have her space, because we knew she was going through it from getting shot, but I had something in the making that I knew would cheer her up.

All I was waiting on was a phone call and I was damn sure getting impatient. We all went back in the kitchen to put our pizzas in the oven. I was so hungry, my stomach was starting to growl like two angry pit bulls. Neither one of us had eaten all day so after ten minutes of watching it cook, we dove in, not once thinking about using the manners of a respectful young lady.

We ate until we felt like whales and then relaxed, watching our favorite movie, *Act Like a Lady, Think Like a Man*, until we couldn't keep our eyelids open. I don't remember how it happened, but the next morning I woke up in my bed naked. The odd part about it was that I wasn't stressing the fact that I was naked. I wanted to know who the hell moved me from the living room couch. I walked to the bathroom to relieve myself, then jumped in the shower. I loved the feeling of the hot water pounding on my body, especially early in the morning when I didn't have to worry about being distracted.

I closed my eyes as the pressure from the spraying shower head found its way between my legs. My body responded faster than my mind being that I hadn't had sex since Doe Boy, which was unpleasant. I tried to think of the last person who had the skills to tame this cat by giving me multiple orgasms from intercourse, and out of all people, Supreme popped in my head.

I smiled to myself and eased my right hand into my wet pussy as I thought of Supreme pulling my left leg over his shoulder while he fucked me standing up against the wall. *Oh shit!* I wanted to scream, but the only sound that came out of my mouth was erotic moans of pleasure. Supreme was stroking in and out of me, rubbing my sensitive clit and playing tag with my G-spot every time he went inside.

"A couple more strokes, baby. I'm almost there," I moaned, not able to keep quiet any longer. I felt the sensation building up deep inside me ready to explode like a weapon of mass destruction. I could tell it was going to be powerful, so like the beast I was, I braced myself for the fifty-foot wave that was about to flow through my body as I steered my surfboard.

*Three...two...one!*

"Excuse me, girl, but I have to use the bathroom bad," Nah Nah shouted, bursting through the door of the bathroom. I jumped to the back of the tub, and covered myself after opening my eyes in shock.

"I'm taking a shower. You couldn't wait until I got out?" I shouted.

"No. I couldn't wait. The bathroom downstairs was too far, and I don't know why you covering yourself like your pussy is made of gold and somebody trying to steal it. I've seen your pussy a million times and last time I checked, it looked just like mine, only difference is you got all that damn hair as a landing strip," she shot back.

I wanted to kill Nah Nah so bad and if I could've just by thinking about it, she would've been a dead bitch. She peed and then tried to talk to me before washing her hands and leaving. I guess my silence told her that I wasn't friendly at that moment. I stayed in the shower a little while longer, washing and rinsing my body before getting out to the cool breeze. Everybody was still asleep, except for Nah Nah I guess, so I moved swiftly as I could without making too much noise. I walked around the whole house naked for about ten minutes giving my pussy a chance to breathe, while I checked on everybody, making sure they didn't have anybody in there with them.

Yeah, that was one of the rules in the house. Everybody had to be advised before you invited a visitor into this house. That's why I had to sneak Hollywood out the last time he came to put that golden head on me. Everything was good in the hood, so I relaxed in the living room. After putting some clothes on, I figured once the girls woke up we all could go on a little shopping spree to spend some of the money we had burning holes in the bottom of our purses.

Two hours later, I was falling back asleep while everybody else was just waking up. I was having a dream that Kayla pushed me in this ocean and I was drowning. I started coughing and spitting up water, everything felt so real. Right when I felt my body sinking deeper and deeper like the *Titanic*, I woke up to find Nah Nah laughing to the point of crying, while standing over me with a pot of cold water in her hand.

"Karma's a bitch, ain't she? That's why I love that hoe," she said and continued laughing.

I wanted to beat her ass, but I didn't because just like karma's a bitch, her sister is the bitch of all bitches.

Shanel and Nicole walked into the bathroom as I was drying myself and just stood there. At first, I wasn't paying them any attention, but after a while, it started aggravating me to the point I wanted to scream. "Why you hoes staring at me?" I asked, with a little attitude in my voice.

"Well, first I wanna say that I saw the look on your face when Nah Nah poured that water on you and you thought you were gone drown. That was some funny shit. I ain't lying," Nicole laughed, then continued. "But Shanel and I was thinking about going shopping and wanted to know if you would like to go?"

When you've been around or known a person for years, it's like you all start thinking the same and even finishing each other's sentences. I hadn't told anybody I wanted to have a girls' day out and go shopping, but somehow, my girls wanted to do the same thing. If that ain't no coincidence, then I don't know what to call it.

"Girl, you might not believe me, but I was just thinking the same thing," I responded.

We all spent thirty minutes getting on fleek and to be honest, I had to say I was looking the flyest in my silver and white dress designed by Tom Ford. My hair rested on my shoulders in light curls. My see-through stilettos complemented my pedicured feet, and my face was make-up free, except for a little lip gloss that left them looking sexy enough to kiss for hours.

Everybody jumped in E'mani's Dodge Magnum once again, but this time, we all had stacks on top of stacks of dead white presidents in our purses. We sashayed through the Millennium

Mall, blowing money like a leaf blower blows leaves. We were so turned up that people started thinking we were celebrities, and two dudes walked up to us and asked for our autographs like straight groupies. We gave it to them, then lied and told them we were a rap group called the Baller Babies, and we had just got signed to a one-album deal with Maybach Music Group.

"You telling me you all know Rick Ross, Meek Mills, and Wale?" they asked, looking more starstruck than ever. We all looked at each other before shaking our heads yes, while trying not to burst into laughter.

"I can't believe this. You don't mind if we be your body-guards and walk you around until you leave?" they asked again. We thought it was hilarious, but you couldn't tell us nothing as we enjoyed our couple hours of fame. We went through store after store and left out with bags on top of bags. Every once in a while, the two dudes would jack somebody up for standing too close to us and we'd have to calm them down by assuring them everything was okay. It was just all too damn fumy. If I'd recorded this whole experience and put it on YouTube, I know I would've reached a million viewers in the first day. Two hours came so damn fast we didn't even realize it, until Nah Nah said something. We let the boys walk us to the car, thanked them and then gave them a thousand dollars apiece, before jumping back on the road and going home.

I swear we had so much stuff that every last one of us had a hard time carrying it into the house. I could literally say we spent close to twenty thousand dollars apiece and that's not counting the money we gave the two groupies. Now tell me that ain't ballin' and I'll tell you to go fuck yourself. After about thirty minutes of putting my things away, I walked downstairs to find everybody stuffing their face with Chinese takeout. You know my greedy ass went off when I didn't see my plate.

"Y'all triflin' ass hoes ordered food and didn't—"

"Your plate is in the oven, so you can stop talking shit," Nicole shouted, cuttin' me off in the middle of my sentence. I smiled before going into the kitchen to get my food and then squeezed between Shanel and Coco, while I cleaned my plate.

"Damn, Sleeping Beauty, about time you got yo' ass up. I thought you was dead up there for a minute," Shanel said to E'mani as she came down the stairs. We all talked and joked with each other, until we wanted to kill E'mani for slapping our tattoos. I couldn't lie, that shit hurt and E'mani knew it, that's why her gap tooth ass was laughing. I hope she knew karma's big sister was waiting on her ass too, just soon as that sling came off.

My cell phone started ringing, causing all of us to jump, because it was on vibrate, but that didn't stop them from wanting to murder E'mani.

"Hello?" I answered, not recognizing the number and from there it's like I blacked out, because all I saw was murder.

## Chapter Seventeen
### E'mani

Do you know how good it feels when you have the power to do what you want and not reap the consequences of it? Yeah, on top of the damn world, that's exactly how I felt at that moment. I knew Mahogany, Nicole, Nah Nah, Coco, and Shanel wanted to get revenge on me, but I was handicapped and that was my get out of jail free card.

We were all still in a full-fledged argument when Mahogany answered her cell phone. I wasn't really paying attention to what she was saying, but her body language told me something wasn't right.

"Hold up! Hold up!" I shouted over all the yelling. Once they caught on to what I was talking about, we all sat quiet, and waited until she ended her call.

"It's that time," she said once she hung up. I didn't know what the hell was going on, but all of a sudden, everybody started scrambling like roaches when a light came on. I watched as they got dressed and headed out the door. I was still sitting on the couch stuck on stupid, not
knowing what to do until Mahogany yelled for me to bring my ass on.

We drove for ten minutes, only stopping once. We made it to our destination, which was an empty farm house. Mahogany led the way to the back, then knocked three times before we were let in. I couldn't believe my eyes when I saw Neeko's naked body tied to a chair, with burn marks all over him. At first, I felt sorry for him and wanted to try and help him escape, but then flashbacks of how he tortured and almost killed me popped into my head once I glanced at my arm in a sling.

"How did you all find him?" I asked.

Mahogany answered simply by saying, "Because he slipped," and then grabbed a gun from one of the two masked men standing next to Neeko.

"E'mani, now I know you're not a killer and you believe in forgiveness, but I want you to think about it real good. This is the same muthafucka who tried to stamp your ass and got your arm in a sling right now. What you gonna do?" she asked, pushing the gun into my hand. I watched as tears ran down Neeko's face, while he begged me to spare his life. I thought about it, but then realized he didn't give a damn about me crying when he was slapping the shit out of me, and now that the shoe is on the other foot, he didn't want to take his consequences like a man. That's a real bitch move, and it pissed me off. I pointed the gun at his head, then walked close enough to where I was at point blank range. He continued to beg me, but the more he did, the madder I became. I wanted him to suffer, I wanted him to feel the pain I felt, fight for his life like he made me do. I wanted it so bad that tears started running down my face as I thought about everything I had been through these last couple weeks.

"Do it, E'mani. Pull the trigger!" I heard somebody yell but couldn't figure out who. I pushed the gun even closer to his head and that's when it happened.

"Do it! Do it! Do it!" I pulled the trigger and held it while I closed my eyes tight until there were no more bullets left to shoot. When I opened my eyes again, I only saw half of Neeko's face on the floor in a puddle of blood. I quickly dropped the gun and ran out the door, in order to catch my breath and control myself from vomiting everywhere. I couldn't believe I had just killed a man, but the adrenaline and energy that flowed through my body felt unreal. It really felt like I had powers and I don't think I ever wanted this feeling to end.

Shanel and Nicole came outside to check on me and make sure I was alright. I assured them that I was actually okay. I just couldn't stand the sight of so much blood.

"Are you sure you're sure?" Nicole questioned some more. "Because I don't want you having bad dreams or telling the wrong person what you did, because you needed to talk to somebody. Let me know what's up right now." I assured her once again and this time she actually believed me. Well, I hope she did.

After about thirty minutes we all jumped back in the car and went home. We rode in silence the whole way, I guess to get our minds right. Well, at least that's what I was doing. I stared out the window at the cats, dogs, birds, and anything else that caught my attention. I just didn't feel like talking.

Once we made it home, I went straight to the bathroom and soaked my body in the tub full of hot water. Today was a day I would never forget. I mean could anybody ever imagine me, E'mani Shanel Newman shooting somebody until they were dead. And I actually didn't feel spooked or paranoid like I thought I would be. I guess revenge really is like the sweetest joy next to getting dick in my case.

I don't know how long I stayed in the tub, but I knew the girls were worried, because it seemed every five minutes, once of them knocked on the door.

"What the fuck do y'all want? Can't you see I don't feel like being fucked with right now?" I yelled at the top of my lungs. I wanted them to hear me and I needed them to understand me.

Once the water started getting cold, I climbed out, grabbed me a towel and then realized I didn't have any clean panties on. I wrapped the towel around me, and walked to my room fast as I could, still trying to avoid everybody. I knew sooner than later, I would have to face them. I couldn't run forever, but until that time came, I guess I'll be by my damn self. I looked myself over in the mirror and clearly saw a different person looking back at me. I no longer saw the image of the innocent woman who grew up in church with her mother. Who I saw staring at me was a person I had never met before, but the craziest part about it was I loved who I had become. She was confident, fearless, and didn't take shit from anybody, the total opposite of the old E'mani.

I threw some clothes on, then walked back downstairs. The whole way there all I could think about was how I fell victim to becoming a Baller Baby. Was that good or bad? That I didn't know, but I would soon find out.

"There go Ms. Gangsta Boo, y'all," Coco shouted as everybody laughed and cheered me on. I was receiving my brownie points for puttin' in that work. I can't lie. They did make me feel good and now I could finally say I gotta body under my belt.

"Y'all are so crazy." I smiled before sitting next to Nicole.

"Coco, I need something to smoke. You got some weed?" They all looked at me in shock like I had a big ass booger in my nose. "What, a bitch can't get high?"

"I know your goody-two-shoes ass ain't talkin' to me. If I pull out my shit you better smoke it or you gone have a hole in your other shoulder," Coco shot back. She left, then came back with a big cigar box full of weed, and five Swisher Sweet blunts. I didn't know how to take the guts out or roll so I just watched until she was done, and then gave it to me to light up. I wanted to show them how the new me rolled, and that I wasn't no lame bitch, so I put the blunt between my lips, lit the tip, and took a long pull like I had been doing this type of shit for years.

"Naw, bitch. Hold that shit in until the blunt gets back to you," Nicole said as I passed it to her. I tried, but by the time she took her second pull, my lungs couldn't take the torture, and I swear I literally coughed up my insides. My chest felt like it was on fire, my eyes started to water, and I couldn't stop myself from coughing up a storm.

Laughing their asses off was an understatement. They were all over each other, and all on the damn floor because of me. I was surprised Shanel brought me a glass of water, but as I drank it, I felt the effect of the weed, alld my head started spinning like a ceiling fan.

"E'mani, you high?" Coco asked after she witnessed the expression on my face. I think I was, but I didn't really know and every time I tried to get up, I would stumble back down.

"My legs feel so light, and it kind of feels like I'm floating or something. What's that mean?"

"Bitch, you high as hell, that's what that mean. Now stay your high ass still and enjoy the blunt before you blow my high," Coco replied.

I hit the blunt again when it came back around to me, this time not so hard, and that's when I realized why the world fought so hard to get it legalized. I felt so damn good. I was laughing at everything, and giggling at everybody.

We enjoyed the rest of the blunt and just sat around the house like zombies. When I say we all were high as the moon, I mean everybody, me, Coco, Mahogany, Nicole, Nah Nah, and Shanel. We looked like real Asians the way our eyes were so low and slanted at the corner. After a while I jumped up and ran to my room to change clothes. I know the girls were wondering what the hell was wrong with me, but I had just remembered I had a doctor's appointment in thirty minutes.

You never know who you might run into when you leave the house, so I had to always be on point and look fly. And that's exactly what I was doing when I slid my sexy legs through my denim skinny jeans and pulled a white blouse over my head with a portrait of Marilyn Monroe on the front. I covered my face with a pair of RayBan shades so my red eyes wouldn't be on display, then walked downstairs and passed the girls.

It wasn't long after I walked through the hospital doors that my name was called to see the doctor. "Good evening, Ms. Newman. I promise you this will not take long. I just needed to see how well your shoulder is healing," Dr. Gray stated as he proceeded to take the sling from around my neck and remove the bandages from my shoulder. I still felt a little pain every now and then, but overall, I was good. He examined my shoulder, squeezed here and there making me jump a little, then spoke. "Well, Ms. Newman, everything seems to be healing wonderfully. Just continue to take it easy, and try to keep that shoulder active to get your strength back. I'll be keeping this and we're all done here," he said, grabbing the sling and walking me to the door.

*Boom! Boom!*

"Nobody move and nobody gets hurt."

I jumped and ran back in Dr. Gray's office as I heard two gun-shots followed by a man's deep voice. *How do I end up in crazy situations like this?* I thought, then hid behind the examining table, praying he didn't come my way. All I could hear was yelling, screaming, and more yelling. I couldn't believe somebody would actually rob a damn hospital, what the fuck would they get? Prescription pills.

## Chapter Eighteen
### Mahogany

*Damn, I ain't never been this muthafuckin' high,* I thought as I sat back on the couch and stared at the ceiling. I was so stuck that I didn't know if I was going or coming. It was like I was stuck between the two.

E'mani had been gone about thirty minutes now, so that meant we had been on this couch for an hour and a half looking stupid.

"Coco, what the hell type of weed was that? That shit got me feelin' too damn high," Nicole asked with a stale look on her face and I could tell she had the cottonmouth. We all gave Coco our undivided attention, because Nicole wasn't the only one who wanted to know.

"I know it's that gas, y'all ain't gotta tell me, but that was some loud laced with a gram of Molly."

"What!" we all shouted at the same time.

"What the fuck you mean laced with a gram of Molly?" Nah Nah finished.

What the fuck was Coco thinking was the only thing that popped in my mind. That bitch just crossed the fuckin' line fa' real.

"Bitch, you just tried us like some fuckin' buddies," Nah Nah said, standing to her feet. "Now if I beat yo' ass, I'll be wrong, but I'm not because you my girl, but that let me know how much you give a fuck about us."

Damn, why it had to happen like this, that shit just blew my high. The silence between all of us caused the moment to become occult, so occult that everybody got up, and went their separate ways without saying a word.

Nah Nah got in her car and left. Coco and Shanel did the same, and Nicole and I left together. I guess we all needed to get away from each other for a while.

I ended up driving until my gas was a little below a quarter-tank, and still ended up nowhere.

"Nicole, you still high?" I asked after stopping at a Shell gas station not too far from the house. She answered, but I couldn't understand nothing she was saying. It sounded as if she was talking with her mouth full, but she wasn't eating anything. She spoke again, this time raising her voice to the point of screaming. I tried to calm her down by grabbing her aim, and holding her still, but then she jumped out the car, stripped down to her panties and bra and ran towards the store, screaming that I was trying to kill her.

"OmiGod!" was all I could say. If I hadn't witnessed this with my own eyes, I wouldn't have believed it. I jumped out the car, and grabbed her before the police had a chance to show up and take her to jail embarrassing all of us. The store clerk was enjoying every last minute of the show Nicole was giving, which explains the big smile he had plastered on his face the whole time.

She came back to her senses after I shook her like a dog would a cat, then forced her back into the car.

"What the fuck is wrong with you?" I said, more to myself than to her. She just looked at me like I was the one who tripped out and ran around half-naked, screaming somebody was trying to kill me.

"Why won't you just let me go? I know what I did was wrong, but I couldn't do it without you. I couldn't be the mother you wanted me to be, so I had to get rid of it. I'm so sorry, baby," she cried. I was so confused because all of this was new information to me, but I could tell she was feeling guilty about what she did. About killing her baby, the baby her husband always wanted.

I hugged her and just listened to her cry, almost crying myself. I couldn't imagine how she was feeling. Knowing her, she wouldn't tell me anyway, just like she never looked for comfort in her girls about the demons she was fighting.

"It'll be alright, just let it all out, girl. I'm here for you." I tried to do the best I could to make her feel safe. I loved Nicole with all my heart and seeing her in pain was the last thing I wanted to view. I reached in the back seat to grab a blanket and wrapped it around her before driving us back home. I was hoping the girls were there, but then again, I didn't know if Nicole was ready to face what happened, because I knew they were going to ask. To my surprise, there were two cars parked in the driveway which belonged to Coco and Shanel.

"What the fuck! I can't believe this shit," I heard them screaming as Nicole and I walked up the driveway. I was wondering what the hell was going on, but the shock didn't come until we walked in the house, and were met with the news that Nah Nah had been killed. At that moment, I felt my whole world crashing in as everything started moving in slow motion and memories of Nah Nah flashed before my eyes. It was like this whole thing was a nightmare that felt real, and couldn't seem to wake up from it.

"Who killed her? Who the fuck killed Nah Nah, huh Shanel?" I asked over and over until she snapped back.

"I don't fuckin' know who killed Nah Nah. I don't fuckin' know," she broke down.

Tears rolled down both of our faces as we embraced each other as if our lives depended on it. Everything was happening so fast. I mean, I just saw her. We smoked and chilled and now she's dead.

We all waited until Nicole threw on some clothes before jumping back in my Beamer and smashing out. I didn't give a fuck if the murder happened in Guam, I was going there. Luckily, we didn't have to go that far, because the parade of police cars led us about two miles from the house. We jumped out the car and played the background, not wanting to be seen and to try and find out as much information as we could.

There were news cameras everywhere, bystanders all over the place, and more police officers then I've ever seen at one time. I tried to get close as I could without causing a scene, but the minute I saw Nah Nah's dead body, I couldn't stop the tears as I cried to myself. She had been shot a total of five times, two in the head and three in the chest. They said a note was left beside her body and as the news reporter read it, I became more confused than ever.

"Surprise, surprise! I know you thought that it was over, but it's not. When E'mani got away, it pissed me off and then you killed Neeko, which angered me more. But I looked at the bigger picture, one down and four more to go. Watch yourself, because I won't stop until every last one of the Baller Babies are dead."

"That was the note left by our mystery killer, and the city police department is asking for help from anybody who can provide information that will lead to the arrest of our killer. Stayed tuned and I will update you with all new leads as they come to us, and remember you heard it here first. I'm Brittany Collins and this is C.F.T.N.S. Central Florida's Trusted News Station."

I just stared, even after the news lady went back to her truck. I had no idea who could have killed Nah Nah, even the hint they gave about being pissed because E'mani got away did no justice. We all knew Neeko was the one who'd kidnapped her and now he's swimming with the fishes so where does that leaves us? Nowhere.

I found Nicole, Shanel, and Coco in the crowd, then hopped in the car before speeding off. I knew they were all feeling some type of way about everything, but I had to be the one to control my emotion, because I had to contact her family to see what they wanted to do about handling the funeral arrangements. That didn't mean whoever killed Nah Nah got away with it, because believe me, they were gone get theirs and you could bet that.

We rode around the city, the song "Live in the Sky" by T.I. and Jamie Foxx playing and just reminisced, well at least that's what I was doing. I was thinking about the first time Nah Nah and I met each other at the Florida Institution for Teenage Girls and instantly bumped heads, because we both wanted to run the whole institution.

My name was already spreading like a wild fire, because I was the new girl and then I had to bust two hoes' asses for stealing my shit. I didn't even know who stole it, I just picked out two girls and beat that ass to set the record straight that I was far from scary and will fight if I had to. That alone got me respect and from then on, I was running things until word got back to Nah Nah, who was the head of the Blood gang.

First, she tried to get me to join her gang, but I refused because I really didn't like running with a group of people. I was an animal by myself, and wasn't trying to take orders from nobody that didn't have on a badge. Then she started sending girls at me, and one by one, I handled my business receiving more wins than losses. This went on until I'd fought every girl screaming, "Suwoo," except for Nah Nah. I felt like a savage beast ready for whatever came my way, but Nah Nah was a smart girl and thought like a leader by befriending me and from there, we were inseparable.

The sound of a horn blowing brought me back to reality as I swerved to the right to prevent rear-ending the car in front of me.

"I'm not trying to be the next one to get killed, so you need to watch what you doing, Mahogany," Nicole said, finally getting her voice back.

I took a quick glance at her and smiled. "My bad, girl, my mind was somewhere else." If she only knew how true that statement was, but then again, I think we all were thinking about Nah Nah in some form, shape, or fashion.

We rode until we were forced to stop in front of a restaurant by the name of Hungry, known for its soul food. The aroma was too strong, and my stomach was so empty. We all sat in a booth far off from the other customers, mainly so we could discuss what our plans were going to be about us making a statement that the Baller Babies were pissed off and was coming for revenge. I wanted so bad to go out and kill everybody I thought had something to do with Nah Nah's murder, but I also knew that wasn't the way to handle things.

"How are you ladies doing? My name is Michael, and I will be your waiter today," a James Brown lookalike stated as we all laughed until tears started racing down our faces.

Keith Williams

## Chapter Nineteen
### E'mani

After about twenty minutes of hiding, I couldn't help myself from being nosey, so I got up to peep around the corner of the door. Everybody was stripped half naked and looked as if they were forcing themselves not to cry. The men stood in their boxers, while the women were in their panties and bras. I wanted to make a run for it towards the door, but knew my clumsy ass wouldn't make it, because the floor would be calling my name.

"Psst...psst...Ms. Newman, what are you doing? They have guns out there," Mr. Gray whispered, trying to get my attention. I heard him, but I acted as if I didn't. I was too busy trying to get away from his crying ass. While I was trying to think of my next move, this grown ass man was literally crying about him not being able to see his wife and kids again. I mean, c'mon! I'm the lady. He's supposed to be the strong man telling me not to cry and that everything was going to be alright, not the other way around.

"I saw two white men, maybe about thirty-five years old, blond hair, about six feet give or take, wearing hand-me-down clothes, reminding me so much of a bum," I said, explaining to the police officer everything I remembered about the suspects in the robbery. I really didn't want to talk to them, because what I was doing at the moment was snitching, but Mr. Gray told them that I saw everything, so they should talk to me.

When I finally did get to leave, I damn near popped a wheelie, burning rubber, trying to get far away as I could from that place. I couldn't wait to get home and tell the girls about my doctor's visit. I know they weren't gone believe me, but I wasn't going to let that stop me from telling my story.

The closer I got to the house, the more police cars I saw. I couldn't really tell what was going on, but from the news vans, and crowd of people standing around, I knew it was something serious.

"Can you all get the fuck out of my way?" I yelled and blew my horn like a mad woman as I tried to turn on my street. The way people looked at me, I could tell they didn't like my attitude, since most of them gave me the finger as I passed, but I didn't give a fuck how any of them felt.

When I did turn into my driveway, I was quickly met by two detectives explaining that there was an armed and dangerous man in the area. They showed me a picture and I think I pissed in my pants right there on the spot.

"Ma'am, his name is Kevin Highway. He's suspected of murder, so we're asking you to be careful and if you happen to see him or anybody that looks like him, give us a call," the taller of the two said, giving me a card with his number on it. I accepted it, then walked towards my front door, still in shock.

My first intention was to call Mahogany and tell her about all this, but the minute I stepped through the threshold, I felt my body being forced to the floor, and a hand covering my mouth. I tried to scream, hoping the two detectives would hear my cries, but I soon realized I was wasting my breath, because the only sound that could be heard was moans.

"Please stop trying to scream. I'm not going to hurt you. I just want to talk to you," I heard my attacker say. I thought about it for a minute, because I really was scared but then again, I thought about what Mahogany had told me he did for us, and that eased my mind a little. I stopped struggling and trying to scream before looking him in the face, as he slowly removed his hand away from my mouth. I stood to my feet, then watched as he stood and from there, he introduced himself.

"I know you don't know me, but I'm a friend of Mahogany's. Everybody calls me Hollywood. I need to talk to her about something important, if you don't mind."

"Well, she's not here, which you probably already know, and before we talk any further, I want to know how you got into my house and why did you tackle me to the floor?" I replied, giving him a hard look. He smiled a little, then apologized for breaking my bedroom window, well Coco's bedroom window. He then followed me to the couch, where he shared with me everything from him and Supreme, to him and Mahogany. I already knew most of everything he told me about Mahogany because she had told me, but it kind of surprised me a little hearing it from him.

"Tell me this, Hollywood, what kind of person fucks his best friend's girlfriend and then kills him because of it?" I asked, wanting to know how he would answer it.

He smiled in a cool mack daddy kind of way, and then licked his lips. "You taking everything I said the wrong way. Yeah, Supreme and I was closer than friends and yeah, I did end up fucking Mahogany, who I didn't know was his ex. Supreme was starting to let his money blind him from the people who really cared about him and that pushed us apart. Now, I know Doe Boy from back in the day, and I was the one who introduced them, so when he called me and offered a hundred thousand for Supreme's head, I took it with no problem. So yes, I did kill him over Mahogany in a way, but I didn't in a way, you feel me?"

I sat there and stared, wondering how he could let pussy come between him and his right-hand man.

"Excuse me, let me know what's on your mind. You just all of a sudden got quiet on me," he said, taking me away from my thoughts.

"I was just wondering...what is taking Mahogany so long to come home," I replied, lying my ass off. I had to think of something real fast, because I knew he didn't want to know what I was really thinking.

I offered him a drink or something to eat to bypass the awkwardness of our conversation, because I really was starting to feel some type of way about him.

"Naw, I'm straight," he answered without looking at me. I continued to the kitchen to make myself a stiff drink, while I processed everything that happened to me today and for some reason, I felt like the worse had yet to come.

I called Mahogany in an attempt to let her know what she had waiting on her when she got home, but all I received was the voicemail, telling me she couldn't make it to the phone, and she might or might not call me back. I had been in the kitchen for a while now and had a feeling that Hollywood would be coming to look for me if I didn't get back to the living room.

"Who were you just talking to?" Hollywood asked, soon as I took the phone from my ear and turned around. I literally almost caught a heart attack when I saw him so close behind me.

"I was trying to call Mahogany, but why is it any of your business?"

"It's my business because I saw that detective give you a business card, and you must've forgot that I'm wanted for murder, so I can't put anything past you or anybody else for that matter," he shot back. I felt where he was coming from, but I would never give him the satisfaction of telling him that to his face, especially in my own house.

"Well, I'm sorry you feel that way, but this is my house, and I will use the phone or anything in it whenever I feel like." He smiled, then calmly walked over to where I was standing and picked up my cell phone, I guess to go over my recent calls. I stood there and watched as he did, not once protesting, because I didn't want him to feel as if I had anything to hide.

Once he realized that he could somewhat trust me, I think I saw a weight being lifted off his shoulders literally. We walked back to the living room, where we relaxed and talked some more about him and Mahogany. He told me how he'd met her at a night club when she told him to eat her pussy while her period was on. I laughed a little even though he wasn't, but that was something I knew Mahogany would do. He then told me he snapped and that's when Nah Nah pulled her gun and threatened to kill him if he didn't calm down.

The thing I couldn't believe was that after everything he went through with Mahogany that night, he still ended up dating her, fucking her or whatever it is they want to call it. I don't get it. He gave me a look that said it wasn't meant for me to understand. It was his life, not mine and at that moment, I felt the same way. I made myself another stiff drink, which had me feeling somewhat tipsy and when I stumbled back into the living room, it was like everything happened within a split second.

Hollywood and I both were staring down the barrel of four semi-automatic handguns, and all I could think about was how they entered the house without us noticing them.

Keith Williams

## Chapter Twenty
### Mahogany

"I say we kill everybody that's a part of Neeko's crew since we don't know which one killed Nah Nah," Coco stated eyeing everybody once the waiter left. I stared back at her, and even though she was somewhat calm, I could tell she was pissed off about Nah Nah.

"Then what? That ain't gone bring her back," Shanel shot back.

"No, but it'll make us feel better knowing justice was served the right way."

I felt where Coco was coming from, but at the same time, Shanel was right, because what's killing people that had nothing to do with Nah Nah's murder going to prove? I want the muthafucka that pulled the damn trigger. At first I wanted to make a statement, but now I gotta do it for my girl, and not just for the Baller Babies.

The waiter finally brought us our orders, and threw in some extra hot sauce for making us wait fifteen minutes longer than everybody else. We all looked at each other, knowing this muthafucka had just tried us, but we let it go. Well, they let it go, not me. I was pissed, and hoped he knew he had just cost himself a hundred-dollar tip.

We all ate until we felt about four months pregnant, and then left without leaving a tip. I made sure of that, even though Shanel dropped thirty dollars as we left. I was quick with my hands, so it ended up in my pocket by the time we made it to the car.

The ride home went smooth and peaceful as we rode in silence to the pleasuring voice of Whitney Houston. That woman had a voice on her. I mean, I truly believe she could solve all the problems in the world for the moment if she performed in front of the White House, or anywhere for that matter. I was enjoying every last minute of this carefree moment, and wished it could last forever but everybody knows nothing lasts forever, especially the Baller Babies, so we wasn't going to fool ourselves in thinking it would.

I turned onto our street and then the driveway before turning the music down. We all got out the car at the same time and headed towards the front door, when Coco's shattered bedroom window caught our attention. We knew this couldn't have been an accident, because the closest house was about a mile away, so if you didn't live here or you weren't a visitor, you had no business on our damn property. One by one we all drew our guns, thinking it could only be one person who would have done this, and that was the bitch who had the balls to murder Nah Nah. I went in first, followed by Nicole, Coco, and then Shanel. Everything looked normal, besides her door being wide open, Coco informed us, but something was definitely wrong. I just didn't know what. I needed more answers, and I had to find them. With our guns still drawn, we made our way downstairs where we ran into the surprise of our lives, well the surprise of my life.

There were two voices coming out of the kitchen, and neither of them sounded familiar. It sounded as if they were coming our way, so with the quickness of a striking rattlesnake, I hid in the hallway closet while Coco, Shanel, and Nicole hid behind the couch. I counted to three after hearing the voices get closer and right as they sat down, I burst through the door, and like always, my girls had my back with their guns in hand, until our eyes landed on E'mani and Hollywood.

"What the hell is going on in here?" I asked as they both stared at us like two curious puppies. I tried to stay in control, but I was so fuckin' confused. Hollywood was the last person I would've thought to be sittin' on my couch right now, especially with E'mani.

"Damn baby, you ain't happy to see me?" he asked and stood to his feet before walking towards me. I raised my gun higher, now aiming directly at his face to stop him where he stood.

"I'm not your baby! No, I'm not happy to see you and if you take one more step, I will blow your fuckin' head off." Everybody stared me down, surprised at what just happened and I couldn't even lie, I was surprised my damn self. After everything I heard about him on the news, he just shows up to my house unannounced and think shit was sweet. He had to be trippin' on Molly.

"I'm about to break everything down to you, so you might wanna listen carefully. I know you killed Supreme, but you pulled a coward ass drive-by and to me, that's some pussy shit. Don't get me wrong now, I'm glad Supreme is dead and by now, I know you've figured out, so is Doe Boy. Two people you had some kind of connection to, so it's only right that you join the both of them in hell." I meant every word I said, and now that he knew it, I couldn't trust him to leave this house alive. I tried counting to ten before I pulled my trigger, but what he said next not only spared his life for the time being, but it caught everybody's undivided attention.

"I know who killed your sista, Nah Nah."

My heart dropped from my chest to the bottom of my feet like it weighed a million pounds. I looked at my girls to see the reaction on their faces, not believing what I had just heard, but they looked just as surprised as I was so I knew he said what I thought he'd said.

"You think this shit is a fuckin' game you play on TV? Man, I swear to God, I will make you watch as I kill your whole damn family, and then kill you if you bullshit me," I yelled at him through clenched teeth while pointing the barrel of my gun damn near in his right eye socket. He kept pleading with me until I was convinced that he really did know something. He kept telling me it was somebody I knew.

After about twenty minutes of getting the details of what Hollywood saw and not the names, we all got strapped like the Russian mob, and drove two cars deep to a place that could easily put you in the mind of hell.

"Where the fuck are we?" I asked, without looking in the backseat at Hollywood. He hesitated for a second, and that was just enough time to see our lives flash before our eyes as bullets flew at us like stones.

"Drive Mahogany, girl. Step on the gas!" E'mani yelled at me. I took my feet off the brake pedal, then hit the gas like I was trying to stomp a deadly spider. I was so damn scared, but I managed to get us out of there. After riding the curbs of two empty highways, I stopped to make sure everybody was alright. "Why the fuck did you stop girl? They gone come after us," E'mani continued shouting.

"Bitch, shut the fuck up! I can't think straight with you yelling at me," I snapped back.

My mind was starting to race a million miles per hour as I jumped out the car, staring at so many bullet holes and my busted out back window. I was really starting to get worried when five minutes passed, and I didn't see Nicole, Shanel, or Coco pull up. *They were supposed to be right behind me*, I thought.

"Where the fuck are they?" I screamed. I felt like I was losing my mind. I was stressin' so bad. I pulled out my cell phone as I paced the road we were parked on, but before I could dial a number, Coco pulled up right next to me, swerving like Boosie Badazz.

"They shot Nicole and she's bleeding real bad!" Coco shouting, jumping out the car before it came to a complete stop. I followed her to the back door, and damn near fainted when I saw Nicole struggling to breathe as her blood soaked the car seat.

"C'mon girl, you gotta fight it. Breathe Nicole, breathe," she tried, but I knew she'd lost the fight when she stopped moving and her eyes rolled in the back of her head. "Nooo! Nicole don't do this. Don't you even thinking about leaving us. C'mon baby, you're stronger than that, don't let it defeat you. Please fight," I yelled, while pushing on her chest like I knew CPR, but her body was motionless. And that's exactly how my life felt as I pulled Hollywood out the car and sent two bullets to his head at point-blank range, killing him instantly.

Coco, Shanel, and E'mani all looked at me like I was crazy, but they didn't understand the demons I was fighting right now. I lost two of my sistas, two of my girls I considered my fuckin' family within ten hours. Can somebody imagine how the fuck I feel? I think I really needed some help to stay sane, because I was about to really lose it. I went back to Nicole's car, kissed her on the forehead, and then closed her eyes before motioning to Coco and Shanel to get in the car.

"You just gone leave her like this?" Shanel asked, while hesitating to walk to my car. I wanted to give this little girl a piece of my mind for asking that dumb ass question, but I took a deep breath, and talked to her as politely as I could.

"What the fuck else can we do, Shanel? If we stay here, then we all going to fuckin' prison. Nicole is already dead. I just shot this nigga in the head and you must've forgot that we have a car full of unregistered guns that have our fingerprints on them."

I let what I told her sink into her little head, then walked to the car as they followed. E'mani took over the driver's seat, so I jumped in on the passenger side and once we were all in, she drove home.

The minute we stepped into the house, I felt a cold chill all over my body. My face was stained with dried tears, and I missed Nah Nah and Nicole as much as I missed my innocent days. I couldn't even walk past their rooms without getting emotional and I had a feeling that would be the thing that would get to me the most.

I settled down after a couple hours by showering and preparing myself something to eat while I watched TV and just as I expected, Brittany Collins from C.F.T.N.S. was telling millions of people that the bodies of Nicole Shipman and Travis Philips were found this afternoon and the police department believes there was foul play involved. I shut the TV off before I started to cry again, and just as I closed my eyes, I received a text message that left me furious.

"You Baller Baby bitches are just too damn easy, but I meant what I said. I won't stop until every last one of you are dead. That's two down now and three more to go."

## Chapter Twenty-One
### E'mani

I laid in bed and just stared at the ceiling, waiting for sleep to come but like any other time, I was going through difficulties in my life, sleep didn't come easy. I really didn't want to blame Mahogany, and the Baller Babies, but it just got where so much shit had gone wrong since I'd met them. I mean, everything, I'd almost gotten killed a million times, everything I touched failed, and I'd gotten so deep that I didn't even know who I was anymore.

I glanced over at my alarm clock, which showed it was 12:36 a.m., then back at the ceiling. I had been laying here for two hours now, and all of a sudden, my mind drifted off to the day I met Boss. Boss was the man I had been seeing for that last couple of weeks. Well, me and Nicole, but it didn't matter to me that she was his main girl, because even though he wasn't a golden head, he had that type of dick that would leave a bitch dick-sick without it. And besides, it ain't the first time I'd shared my man with another bitch. Just ask Mahogany.

Boss was a well put together man that kept a low cut Caesar, and had perfect straight teeth. He stood about five foot ten, and had a tight muscular body that put you in the mind of LL Cool J in his prime. He was my boo thing.

I was thinking about when I met him inside a Victoria's Secret store, and he asked if I would help him find something nice for the special person in his life. I told him I would and pointed him to the lingerie section, where he then asked my bra and panties size, saying she was built like me. I can't lie, at first, I was a little embarrassed by telling a complete stranger the size of my panties and bra, but I quickly shook it off and confidently said, "A size thirty-four-D bra and size eight panties. Well, he ended up buying this really cute and sexy two-piece, lace baby blue set with pink trimming that would make any woman want to show it off. To my surprise, he bought me one too and from there, we made history.

I tried again to get some sleep, but my mind kept bringing me back to Boss and this time, I could feel myself getting moist. I slowly slid my shorts and panties down my legs in one swift motion. My iPod was playing slow jams by R. Kelly and as my thighs separated my hand became one with my kitty. I massaged my clit and fantasized about Boss eating my pussy with his long wet tongue, the way he slowly sucked my thick lips in between his and then looked me in the eyes as his tongue played tag with my clit, causing me to explode like a bomb. *OhmiGod*, I wanted to scream, but I bit down on the pillow instead. My climax lasted a good three minutes, and within no time, he was giving me a free ticket to heaven as he slid his dick so deep inside me, I thought I felt it in my chest. I closed my eyes, enjoying the moment and wishing it would last forever. Then at exactly one thirty, he came inside me as I coated his dick with my own juices, and then fell asleep in his arms.

The next morning, I woke up and caught Mahogany on her way out. The unit on her face told me she was pissed off, and knowing everything that had been going on in this house, I gave Mahogany her space and watched her walk out the door without saying a word.

Even though my life had done a complete one-eighty, I was still my mother's child so whenever there's a problem, I find myself trying to fix it. Like the one we had in this house. I thought it was me that somebody was trying to kill, but after everything that had happened, I now knew they were after the Baller Babies.

I continued to the kitchen after watching Mahogany get into her car and leave. I really didn't know what I was looking for, but I searched the drawers and kitchen cabinets like an officer with a search warrant. I searched for a whole thirty minutes, coming up with nothing. I was tired, hungry and feeling like I was losing my mind, like Young Jeezy.

"What the hell is wrong with me!" I whispered to myself as I sat in the middle of the kitchen floor Indian style, and looked around. I looked around, still not knowing what I was looking for, until my eyes landed on the open cabinet under the sink. I walked towards it and the little black book inside caused my breath to get caught in my throat when I realized what it was.

How long had it been there? Who all knew it was there? And how many of the girls had read it? Those were the thoughts that had me hugging the book as if somebody was after it, while looking around. I ran back to my room taking the stairs two at a time, then closed and locked my door, making sure it was secured before sitting on the bed with my back against the headboard. I could feel my hands sweating as a sign of me being nervous, but I took a deep breath and opened it before reading.

*Tuesday, June 5, 2018*
*9:15 p.m.*
*"Sex My Mind"*

*It's impossible to love me until you've made love to my mind. Not physically, but mentally. Sex my mind until I lose track of time and want you in the worse way until my body says okay. Tell me your goals, your dreams, your ideas and the little everyday things that make you laugh. Can you do that for me or do you only have enough love to share physically. Sex my mind with the roughness of a raging bull, and the speed of a soaring dove. Is that too much of me to ask for, because my mind is really without love?*

*V Mani V*

I smiled as tears started falling down my face. So many memories flooded my mind at once that my emotions completely ran wild. I remembered the reason I wrote it and the emotions I was feeling and every time Supreme stayed in the streets twenty-four-seven, only coming to see me when he wanted to fuck me. I mean, the money was always good, but there's more to a relationship than that. I really saw Supreme and I going to the next level as in marriage and kids, but a girl can only take so much. His goals were always his goals, his dreams were always his dreams, in which I mean he was afraid to confide in me, and tell me what was on his heart and mind. I wiped away my tears, cherishing the moments of my past and then turned the pages to continue reading, and hoping not to shed any more tears.

*Sunday, June 10, 2018*
*10:48 p.m.*
*"Hopes and Fantasies"*

*Would you ever tell me your fantasies? I would hope it involves you and I sexing and sucking each other until the sun rises licking our naked bodies. Don't be embarrassed because I want what you want. Sucking, fucking, pulling, and drilling. I hope that's your fantasy. If not, then I hope you want what I want, because it's damn sure close to mine. I need you to wake up and smell the coffee, because it's the new day and age where your wildest fantasies can have your woman begging you for days. Hint, hint. So, while you're loving me, think about my hopes and fantasies.*

*V Mani V*

By the time we broke up, Supreme still hadn't opened up to me. I really wanted to explore more with him, but I guess my innocent ways blinded his vision from really seeing the freak in me. He wouldn't even let me perform oral sex on him. I mean, everybody knew I wasn't a golden head, but I wanted to try something new and while I was at it, please my man.

I stared at the page for a while reminiscing of the times my mind went wild with erotic fantasies. I kept reading the same poem over and over again. When I finally caught myself and came back to reality, I started to get up thinking that was enough for now. The farther away I went from the book, the more I wanted to continue reading. I debated with myself saying I would only read one more poem, and just to keep it honest with myself, I opened the book back up and only read one more poem.

*Saturday, June 25, 2018*
*10:20 p.m.*
*"Passionate Words"*

*How powerful would your emotions be if I spoke passionate*
*words to you. Love, loyalty, honor, and respect. Let me take you to*
*a place that's more beautiful than Heaven, but also peaceful, then*
*Earth, where don't nothing matter, but how much you mean to me.*
*Passionate words!*
*Mentally, physically, spiritually and emotionally, I can take*
*you there. Yes, I mean every word I say, but at the same time, I*
*hope you recognize my passionate words. To my king, if you are,*
*I'm ready to start our royal family.*

*V Mani V*

This last poem really brought back a lot of emotion. At that
time in my life, I felt like Supreme meant more to me than my
own life. If he said jump, my only reply would be how high. If he
told me to lick his body clean after he had just got done working
out, I would only tell him to make sure he has a towel to dry up all
the saliva I may leave behind. I was what most people call sprung,
yes sprung over the dick, and if the situation with Mahogany
hadn't presented itself, I most likely still would have been.

I jumped up out the bed to put the book in my top drawer for
safekeeping. Nobody had no business in my room so I didn't think
it would be a problem keeping it there. I then looked myself over
in the mirror, making sure my face wasn't streaked with tears and
walked back downstairs. I didn't really know if Coco or Shanel
had woke up yet, so I moved quietly as I could to prevent them
from going off on me. But soon as I reached Shanel's room, I
couldn't stop myself from screaming and yelling at the top of my
lungs, "What the fuck is going on? Girl, ohmifuckin' God!"

Keith Williams

## Chapter Twenty-Two
### Mahogany

I tried almost a hundred times to call that number back, but it always said the same thing. "You have reached a number that is not accepting calls at this time." I was boiling with anger, but there was nothing I could really do at that time so after thirty minutes, I finally forced myself to sleep.

The next morning, I woke up bright and early, took a shower, and jumped in my Beamer.

E'mani was the only one up at the time, but I was on a mission so I had to shoot her a dagger to keep her from asking me a million questions about where I was going.

"Welcome to Metro PCS. May I offer you my service?" a white girl with blonde hair and breasts the size of watermelons asked soon as I stepped through the door. Now, I wasn't gay, bisexual, or even confused, but her breasts really caught my attention. I felt like a man staring at them big things, and when she caught me, my face was flushed with embarrassment.

"I am so sorry," I said softly.

"It's okay. I get that a lot. With the size of these things, you could imagine how much attention I get from men and women," she said, cutting her eyes at me and then smiling.

After introducing ourselves, I gave Jamie my cell phone and asked if she could get a name and address from the number of the last text message I received. At first she said no and that it was against store policy, but once I slipped her a hundred-dollar-bill, she quickly took my phone and excused herself to the back.

While she was gone, I browsed around at some of the new phones and tablets they had to offer. Most of them were on fleek, but I had to get my mind right quick, because that wasn't the reason I was there.

Twenty minutes passed, and I was starting to get worried until I saw her walking my way.

"I have good news, and bad news. Which would you like to hear first?" she asked once we were face-to-face. I hated the fact that there was bad news and to be honest, I'd rather there not be, but there was, so that's what I wanted to hear.

"The bad news is that the number is under the name Freeway Ricky Ross, which is an infamous drug lord from the late 80s." I thought about it, and tried to think of anybody I knew who used names of drug lords, but I kept coming up with nothing. She then stared waiting for the sign that I was ready for the good news. Once I thought about it a little more, I told her to go ahead.

"The good news is that I have an address that's not too far from here. Would you like me to come with you when I get off work? I know how it is when you have women calling and texting you about your man," she asked. It was really nice of her to want to help me, but this was some deep shit. And a white girl like her will only get herself stamped trying to be Super-Save-A-Hoe. I smiled then shook my head slowly before getting the address and walking back to my car.

I thought hard on my way home about how I was going to handle this situation. God knows I didn't want to make the same mistake as before and lose another one of my girls. The whole thought of that just made me emotional. So I did something I would've never in a million years thought of doing. I prayed to God. I prayed until tears started falling down my face, asking God to keep me and my girls safe from the wicked families that would try to harm us. I never believed in catching the Holy Ghost, but at the moment, I could feel I was being protected and that somebody above was watching over me. When I parked in my driveway, I left the car and ran into the house to get the girls so they could ride with me to handle this bullshit. Making my bird call was all I planned on doing when I got in the house, but the sight of E'mani and Shanel going blow for blow caught me by surprise. I damn near pissed on myself from laughing so hard. Now, E'mani wasn't a fighter, but she was doing more than just the windmill. I mean, she was throwing her hands like she sparred with Lala Ali, but she couldn't fuck with Shanel, who knocked her on her ass not once, but two times as she kept getting back up.

"Hold up! Hold up! That's a God damn 'nough. What the fuck is going on in here?" I asked as I stood between the both of them. They both tried to talk at the same time, which only made it harder for me to understand, and I wasn't trying to hear it.

"Okay! Okay! Okay! I know I have two ears, but I can only understand one person at a time so can you please stop screaming?" I pleaded.

By this time Coco was coming down the stairs with a blunt in her mouth like she had no worries. I wanted to tell her about her ass, because here is her sister fighting with E'mani and she did nothing to stop it. We supposed to be family. I let it go, because we had bigger problems then whatever they were in here fighting about.

"What's going on?" Coco asked, in between taking a pull of her blunt. I looked at her with disgust, because I wanted to bash her fuckin' head in, acting like she didn't know what was up.

I ignored her question, and then brought them up to date about our other situation. "I'm going to need for you all to listen to me, and listen good. I received a text last night from Nah Nah and Nicole's killer." All three of them looked as if I had just told them I was HIV positive, and planned on spreading the shit. "Whoever it is, is trying to kill all of us and won't stop until they do, but the good thing is, we have a chance to get their ass first. I went to Metro and got a name and address for the number that texted me last night, and lucky for us, it ain't too far, but we all have to be on point at all times, because I can't stand to lose any of you." They all shook their heads up and down, letting me know they understood what I was saying. I then told them about me praying and just like I expected, neither of them could believe it, but I assured them that it happened, and even suggested we pray together before we made our move.

E'mani took over and said a prayer that had all of us teary-eyed. We couldn't help it and the way our lives were going, we needed to change so we all put our two cents in and promised God that after this was over, we would change our lives and start showing Him the attention He deserved.

After we wiped the tears from our faces, we embraced each other in a big group hug and kisses on the cheek. We really didn't know how everything was going to play out, but either way this was the beginning of a new life for us. We all separated and went to our rooms to get dressed in our kick ass gear or monkey suit, however you wanna say it.

"E'mani, Coco, and Shanel! I hope y'all hoes ready," I yelled out after about twenty minutes of wrapping my hair, throwing on a black blouse, black shorts, black shades, and a black fitted cap. I was ready. No questions asked. This was the moment I had been waiting for.

The girls came down the stairs and I couldn't lie, they were ready too, especially E'mani with her two chrome deuce fives in her hands.

"Girl, where the fuck yo' ass get them from?" I asked, loving the way they shined in her hands.

"I got connections. The plug fuck with a bitch the long way, that's where I get them from," she answered, trying not to laugh. We all burst into laughter, because it was funny hearing E'mani's green ass talkin' gangsta.

"Bitch, shut yo' green ass up before we leave you here, and tell the plug that," I shot back at her. She frowned up her face like she had just ate a lemon, honestly, I didn't give a fuck. See, where I'm from you can't be softhearted, because everybody around you talks real aggressive. I'm talking about to the point where you feel like their disrepecting you, but they're not. So, I knew E'mani felt some type of way from the way I was talking to her, but she'd been around me long enough, and should have known this was the way I talk, and I wasn't changing it for no fucking body, period.

After a couple minutes we all walked outside to hop back in my old white Honda Accord. Yeah, the same one I used to take trips to ATL when I was trafficking Supreme's dope. She was old, but my baby came through for me every time I needed her and besides, my Beamer was still in the shop getting the bullet holes repaired. We drove the three miles it took and ended up in front of a large building full of wood boxes, reminding me of a warehouse.

We still hadn't gotten out the car yet but could see through the dirty windows when we squinted our eyes.

"What's the plan?" Coco asked as everybody's attention focused on me. I really didn't have a plan so we would have to freestyle it, but best believe I wasn't lettin' them know that.

"This how it's gone go. Coco and I will go in, and kill this bitch or beat her ass, and then kill her ass if we have to. E'mani, you and Shanel stay in the car and make sure everything is Gucci out here. But if we're not out of there in twenty minutes, bring y'all asses in with your guns blazin'. Everybody got that?"

E'mani wanted to say something, but I stopped her. We didn't have time for the bullshit. All I needed to know was do everybody understand. I guess what was understood didn't need to be explained, because silence took over the car while everybody continued to give me their undivided attention.

Since that was out of the way, I popped open the glove compartment and then the center console to grab the three nine millimeters and two snub-nosed .44 Bulldogs.

"Take this, Shanel, and make sure the clip is full before you leave the car. Keep your eyes open, watch each other's back, and remember, it's double B's for life," I said, handing her one of the nines I had. I really wanted this whole thing to be over with, so I was more eager than anyone to get it done. Once I gave Coco the two .44 Bulldogs, we both jumped out the car with one thing on our minds, and that was killing the bitch who killed our girls.

## Chapter Twenty-Three
### E'mani

Shanel was literally hanging from the ceiling by her neck. I mean, to the point of choking and about to pass the fuck out. I didn't know what to do, but I knew I wasn't going to sit there and let her die like a coward. I took one more look at her, then ran fast as I could to the kitchen to get a knife. When I got back, her eyes were beginning to roll in the back of her head.

"Hold on, Shanel," I said as I cut the cord she had wrapped around her neck. She fell kind of hard and I was worried she might've been hurt, until she leaped at me like a hungry lion.

All I could see was stars as she threw blow after blow at my face. I tried holding her, but it was no use. The more I tried, the more my head was used as a punching bag. The knife had fallen to the floor. I didn't know how long ago and since I didn't have anything to protect myself, I took off running downstairs. To my surprise, she was right behind me and when I tripped, I thought it was over for me.

"Shanel, what are you doing? Stop! Please stop!" I yelled, pleading for my life.

"Get yo' ass up and fight, bitch," she snapped, before taking a couple steps backwards.

Again, I didn't know what to do. I didn't want to fight, but if I didn't, she would keep beating me up, so without really thinking, I stood to my feet, and started swinging punches like my life depended on it. Now we were going blow for blow, and even though I was handling my business, Shanel knocked my ass down not once, but twice, and both times I got back up. I was determined to show her that I was not afraid, and she was going to start respecting me.

"Hold up! Hold up! That's a goddamn 'nough. What the fuck is going on in here?" Mahogany shouted, stepping between us, and holding me back.

I tried to tell her what was going on, but every time I started so did Shanel, and all we were doing was yelling at each other.

"Okay! Okay! I know I have two ears, but I can only under-stand one person at a time, so can you all please stop screaming?"

I started to say fuck it, and go back to my room, but the way Coco came downstairs like she was the fuckin' queen of the earth really got under my skin.

Mahogany started talking again and to be honest, I was block-ing everything she said out until I heard her say she received a text from the person that killed Nah Nah and Nicole.

I still didn't get what the hell this bitch was trying to prove by killing us. I mean, we probably didn't even know the bitch.

After Mahogany put us up on game, I went to my room to get ready, and when I say I came for war, the whole muthafuckin' world better believe I came for war. I threw on my black thermal top and bottom, some black pants and blouse, and a black Robbins snapback. I looked in the mirror after I heard Mahogany scream my name to make sure everything was right, but I kept feeling like I was missing something once I ran my eyes over my room. I stopped on my dresser, and went straight to it as I grabbed my twin deuce five. Now I'm ready I thought. I walked back down-stairs to meet the girls who were looking like they were going to take over the fuckin' world.

Once we got to the spot, and Mahogany gave Shanel a nine millimeter before getting out after Coco. I wanted to shoot Shanel in her fuckin' head. I hoped she didn't forget how she tried me earlier when I was trying to help her stupid ass.

"I hope you know when all this shit is over with, I'm gone kick your ass for trying me," I told her while focusing my attention out the window.

She laughed a light chuckle, "Anytime, anyplace, bitch. And for the record, I never liked your scary ass anyway."

"We'll see," I shot back, still staring out the window, but deep down inside her comment cut me to the bone. I never knew she felt like that all this time, and it had to take this situation to show me that Shanel was more like Coco than everybody thought.

Ten minutes passed, and I jumped out the car to get away from Shanel. The tension between us was beginning to get so thick that I was about to suffocate just from sittin' next to her.

I went to the side of the building with both of my guns out. I can't lie I was afraid, but at the same time, I was ready to put every bullet in my magazine in somebody's ass. I tried to look inside the window to see what was going on, but I was an inch too short, and didn't want to jump, because my clumsy ass would. probably attract the bitch straight to me. So, I went around to the first door I saw, which was guarded by a man who could easily have been mistaken for the UFC fighter, Kimbo Slice.

"Excuse me, my car just broke down in front of your building, and I really don't know what to do. Would you mind helping me please?" I asked with a little more sexiness in my voice.

Obviously, I still had it going on, because he willingly left his post with a big smile, and soon as he turned his back to me I put a bullet in the back of his head without thinking twice.

Once he hit the ground, I politely took the gun out of his holster, and tucked it into my waist before relieving him of his keys. "I don't see why men let the pretty face and sweet voice trick them every time," I said while laughing.

Mahogany and Coco had only been in there for a couple minutes so I figured I had a little time to check on Shanel before I played Super-Save-A-Hoe. She was playing with the magazine of her gun when I walked up to the car, loading and unloading, I had a clear view of her and every second I spent standing there, I wanted to send two bullets to her head, and walk off.

Nobody would know. I pulled my gun so that it was level with the window, while contemplating my next move. I was thinking about following my first thought, but after a minute, I decided against it.

The gun was still in my hand, but in the blink of an eye, Shanel looked up to see the barrel of my pistol. I tried to conceal it before she loaded a bullet into the chamber, but the thought of her laughing while standing over my lifeless body caused me to send bullets flying through the window, and into her face. I ran back towards the building after five shots, not waiting to see if she was dead or not.

If she was, I didn't give a damn, the bitch never liked me anyway. She said that out of her own mouth. I had to stop when I got close enough to the back door. My breathing had become shallow, my heart was beating louder than thunder, and everything I had eaten earlier was being forced out of my body through my mouth. What did I just do? I thought . Part of me really felt bad about what I just did, but the other part was saying, fuck her.

"OhmiGod!" I took four deep breaths to calm myself down before straightening up, and wiping my face with my shirt. I had to go check on Mahogany and Coco. They had been in there too long, and it would kill me if something happened to them too. I walked through the door with my guns still drawn. After unlocking it, my vision had to adjust to the darkness, but no matter how much I tried to tell myself that I was in control, I was spooked from the thought of somebody killing me.

The building was huge, and I didn't know where the hell I was going as I walked around looking for Mahogany and Coco. I made so many left and right turns, and still didn't get too far from where I'd started, because I saw the same door I came in through. "Damn!" I shouted getting aggravated with myself. I wanted to give up so bad that it didn't even make sense to keep going.

I stood there for a minute, not knowing what else to do, but trying to come up with something. I heard two female voices, but didn't know if they belonged to Mahogany or Coco. The way things were though, I was about to find out, so I followed them towards the staircase going to the second level of the building. The closer I came to the top of the steps the louder the voices were to me. I took them two at a time, but something inside of me was afraid of what or who I might see.

"Bitch, you're so fuckin' cutthroat, but then again, I should've known it was coming. Pussy-eating-ass hoe, you always hated on us," I heard somebody shout, clearly disappointed. I kept going until I reached the top, and got the surprise of my fuckin' life.

Mahogany and Coco were both tied to a chair by their arms and legs, while Kayla stood in front of them with a gun in her hand and a big smile on her face. I couldn't believe what the fuck I was seeing, not Kayla. That can't be her with a gun in her hand, threatening to kill Mahogany and Coco. Seeing all this made me think back to the day I was in the salon when Neeko tried to kill me. The person wearing the hoodie with the nude picture of us had to be Kayla. At the time, I couldn't imagine her ever doing something like that, but after witnessing what was going on right in front of my face, I was more convinced than ever.

"Damn, I shoulda told Mahogany I thought Kayla had something to do with Neeko and his crew. Maybe I could've prevented this from going down like this," I said, beating myself up for keeping my mouth closed and not telling somebody. I tried to get closer without being noticed, but I was scared shitless, and at the same time, they were exactly in the middle of the fuckin' floor, Wwide the fuck open.

I shifted a little to get comfortable where I was squatted down, because the way things were going I knew I would probably be there until I built up the courage to do something to help my girls. I guess the old E'mani had returned.

## Chapter Twenty-Four
### Mahogany

Soon as we stepped through the front door of the building, my girl Coco shot the first muthafucka we saw moving, which was a tall, lanky Wiz Kalifa lookin' muthafucka.

We came to handle business, so all the extra shit was out the window. Coco was ready to die, and I damn sure was too, to get revenge and kill the bitch who cost the Baller Babies so much pain.

We stripped him of his gun, then got prepared for the parade of so-called killers they had running around as security, but nobody showed up, and that kind of got me to thinking. After hearing that loud ass gunshot, nobody ran to see what was going on. That was crazy. We proceeded on our way, and then separated once we got to the staircase.

"Listen, Coco. Both these staircases lead to the same place. What I need you to do is take that side while I go this way, so we'll have a better chance at catching her by surprise," I said, while doing sign language like the SWAT team does when they're about to do a bust. She agreed without any protest and I was happy, because we really didn't need too much talking going on when it was business to be handled. I tiptoed up the stairs trying not to make any noise. I really wanted this bad, so bad that I didn't even care if my life was also taken in the process.

"Bitch, do it right and don't fuckin' play with me," I heard a female shout, the closer I came to reaching the top. I kept going until I reached the top, and what I saw next didn't even surprise me. After all the shit I'd seen in my lifetime, I took this sight like a shot of gin with no chaser. Kayla had her face deep between the legs of the chick she was with, the last time she tried that gay shit at our house. Yeah, she was eating her lover's pussy like she was dying from hunger. I stood there and watched undetected, while Kayla's tongue repeatedly boxed her lover's clit, drawing moans of pleasure from her mouth. She then slowly slipped two fingers into her lover's pussy, and continued stroking her G-spot over and

175

over. Her moans got louder, her pussy got wetter, and the force she used to pull Kayla's face deeper to her pussy was supernatural, as evidence of her orgasm caused my panties to dampen.

*Damn, I'm trippin'*, I thought as I looked up to see Coco staring at me, eyes bulging out of her head. The signs she was giving me were useless because I couldn't understand her, but the minute I did get a glimpse of what she was trying to tell me, it was too late. The cold steel was already at the back of my head. I stole a look at Coco again, and that's when I realized she too was standing there at gunpoint.

They made us stand there and watch until the show was over before they announced our presence to Kayla and her lover.

"Well, well, well, if it isn't the baller bitches," Kayla's bitch stated. Kayla just stood there smiling as she witnessed the dagger I was shooting at her. I really wish I would've shot both of them bitches in the head soon as I saw them eating each other's pussies.

They tied both Coco and me to a chair, while they figured out what they wanted to do with us. At least, that's what they said. I sat there boiling on the inside as I stared at Kayla. I just couldn't believe this bitch. "Bitch, you're so fuckin' cutthroat, but then again, I shoulda known it was coming. Pussy-eating-ass hoe, you always hated on us," I said meaning every word. I was waiting on Kayla to respond, but the minute she started, she was cut off.

"You brought this on yourself, so you need to stop complaining, and die like the gangsta bitch you was. I told you that I wasn't going to stop killing until every one of the baller bitches was dead. Well, by you coming to my place, you made this shit too easy."

"Who the fuck are you?" I asked as she finished her lil' speech. The more she spoke, the more I stared at her, because she was looking too damn familiar.

She smiled as if I was making a joke, then just as quickly got serious. "You really don't know who I am, I see. Well let's refresh your mind. My name's Ja'mya. Yeah, Supreme's baby sister, only difference is that I'm not a baby anymore. Ever since you and the Baller Baby bitches killed my brother, I made a promise to myself that I would kill every last one of you, even if it meant me dying in the process. My brother was all the family I had left, and you took him from me. Do you know the struggle I went through to survive after you killed him? There was no money left behind for me, and all of his so-called friends only tried to help so they could fuck me."

I smiled, and gave her a view of my gold teeth just to piss her off, but deep down inside I was beating myself up for not recognizing who she was the first time I saw her. It couldn't have been that long and the way her body matured she had to be 'bout nineteen or twenty years old now, but again, how the fuck did I not remember that bitch? Damn, I was slippin'.

The two dudes who had Coco and me at gunpoint left out at that point, but the way my mind was racing, I never noticed until the sound of Ja'mya's voice brought me back to reality.

"Why did you have my brother killed? I mean, all those years you two were together, I know you had to love him," she reasoned.

What did this young bitch know about love, and why is she talking to me? It would be better if she stopped wasting time and got it over with. Then again, another option popped in my head, and I decided to have a little fun before I was killed. "Do you really wanna know why I had Supreme killed?" I asked, but she didn't respond so I continued. "Your brother was a snake. Just like the bitch standing beside you. He didn't understand what loyalty meant, but preached it as if he was a preacher. He treated everybody like a pawn and after he used you for whatever reason, he tossed you to the side, because then you were no longer needed. Everybody he so-called loved, he betrayed them. Me, E'mani, shit, he damn near had another family with her, and even his right-hand man, Hollywood. So, fuck that nigga Supreme and I hope his soul burn in hell." I knew what I said would get her hot as burning coal, but what I didn't expect was what happened next.

Ja'mya slammed the butt of her gun repeatedly into my face, drawing blood instantly. I didn't even scream, because if I was going to die today, I wanted to die an honorable death like the gangsta bitch I was, and not begging for my life like a coward.

She finally stopped and through my blood streaked face, I could see the fire in Coco's eyes. I could tell she wanted to kill Ja'mya and Kayla as much as I did, and seeing her like that only gave me the willpower to survive any punishment I might endure.

Ja'mya stepped back and looked at me, admiring her work like she had put so much time and effort into it, and was proud of what she created. "You know what? I'm not even going to kill you like I did them other two bitches. You're different, and you're the one that caused me so much pain. Killing you right away is nothing. I want to see you scream and beg me for your life, right before I kill you. I want this other bitch beside you to watch, knowing she can't do anything to save the precious Mahogany," she said seething hatred in her eyes.

I smiled, knowing all too well that Ja'mya was not a killer. If she was in fact the one who killed Nah Nah and Nicole, she did it out of hurt for her brother, but now she was wasting too much time, and one thing a person should always remember is when somebody's back's against the wall, they'll do almost anything to come out on top.

Coco and I were basically tied together, and while Kayla acted so smitten and hung onto Ja'mya's every word, I was trying to pull a trick from out my sleeve. I was pulling at the thick rope they had us bound with, but to no avail. I couldn't free us. At one point, I heard Kayla and Ja'mya snickering and thought they had caught me, but I got a hell of a surprise when Kayla walked towards me, wiped my face of the blood Ja'mya caused, then kissed me in the mouth. I'm talking about tongue and all. The only thing I could do was turn my head, but the end of that came when she held me by the face and forced another kiss on me, this time more passionately.

"I've been wanting to do that since the day you walked in on Ja'mya and I fucking on the couch that day. The way your pussy poked out like a peach, I swear I wanted to eat that shit the whole time you watched us," Kayla said with a lustful look on her face.

I wanted to scream and fight so bad, but my face was hurting like hell. I cursed her ass out and called her everything but the child of God, while shooting daggers at her.

She just smiled, pissing me off more and at the drop of a dime, she and Ja'mya were all over Coco and me. Kissing us, ripping our clothes off, and unbuckling my shorts to get to my pink pussy.

Despite the pain I was feeling in my face, I screamed at the top of my lungs and tried to fight like my life depended on it, because it did. I could hear Coco screaming and cursing and when I turned to look her way, Ja'mya had her damn near naked.

Kayla had retrieved the gun from Ja'mya, so I was kind of worried she might shoot me, but the minute I felt her tongue on my pussy, I went crazy, kicking and screaming, yelling as my mind drifted back to my childhood, when my cousin Shay took advantage of my young body and raped me.

In the midst of everything going on, I heard a single shot that left my ears ringing.

## Chapter Twenty-Five
### E'mani

I stayed where I was until I saw two men coming down the same steps I went up. I knew before I did anything I would have to get rid of them, so I followed close behind until I was able to shoot them both in the head without alarming the other.

Well, that plan was easier said than done. When the first one took a bullet to the back of his head, his friend dove for cover and unholstered his gun. For every shot I delivered, he sent back two, making his gun roar like something out of the movie, *Terminator*.

We went back and forward, only coming to an end when I fired my nineteenth shot. I then walked out in the open with my gun still aimed at him. He followed and the second he thought he had the ups on me, he pulled his trigger, only to hear it click. "That's seventeen shots. Sorry for the wait," I stated, before filling his body with lead.

I didn't know how many more people Kayla had working for her, but I knew I had to help Mahogany and Coco before I ran into a situation I wouldn't be able to make it out of.

Two at a time, I ran back up the steps to find Mahogany getting molested by a raging Kayla. Gun still in her hand, Kayla had her face buried deep between Mahogany's legs eating her like it was her last meal. Mahogany screamed and yelled as if she was getting tortured and threw off my concentration, but the moment Kayla came up for air, I pulled the trigger, sending a bullet right to her head. The whole room became quiet as all eyes were now on me, the woman with the smoking gun. I trained my gun on the other woman as she reminded me of a shell-shocked teenager who had just witnessed her mother get killed.

"Kill that bitch, E'mani!" Mahogany screamed. "She's the reason for you getting shot. She sent Neeko to kill you."

I thought for a second, wondering why she would want me dead. She didn't even know me. I guess it was written all over my face, because I didn't even have a chance to ask before Mahogany answered. "She's Supreme's sister, and she thinks the Baller Babies had him killed."

That caught me completely by surprise and to this day, I don't think anybody but Ashlyn and Alice even knew I had something to do with that. I looked at her again and could tell she was afraid. She didn't want to die, and who was I to take her life from her? She was only trying to get justice for what happened to her brother. That's the only reason she sent Neeko to kill me. I can't blame her for that, and I couldn't kill her for it either, so I told her to untie Mahogany and Coco.

Once she did, Mahogany wasted no time showering her with blows that sounded more like gunshots. She tried to fight back, but to no avail could she roll with the punches. I wanted to stop them as I screamed for Mahogany to chill out, but the minute I stepped within arm's reach, Mahogany snatched the gun out of my hand. She shot Ja'mya four times, then finished her once she hit the ground by firing at her body until the gun clicked, indicating that there were no more bullets to shoot.

I turned my head, not wanting to see the dead body. She was so young, and even though she was capable of taking somebody's life, she didn't deserve to die like that.

"She was only a baby, Mahogany. You didn't have to kill her," I cried as the tears rolled down my face freely.

"Bitch, shut the fuck up," she shot back, clearly angry. "If I wouldn't have killed her and that little bitch was presented with a chance to kill us, guess what she would have done? Murder our asses so fuck that shit you talkin' bout with your soft-hearted ass."

Honestly, everybody knew I had a kind heart, but it really got under my skin the way Mahogany was talking to me. She had a way of talking to people like they were beneath her and I knew that, so I let it go, because I knew she was really upset. I watched and waited as they got dressed before we walked downstairs, and to the car. Thankfully, we didn't run into any more problems on our way, but nothing could've prepared me for what happened when we finally did reach the car.

"Omifuckin' God! Not my sister, please God no," Coco screamed once she saw the dead body of her twin sister. She broke down, and cried like I'd never seen before, and not once did I try to comfort her. Deep down in my heart, I was surprised I didn't feel any guilt, but I felt like my back was against the wall and I did what I thought was right. Even though she wasn't really good at it, at some point Mahogany went over to comfort Coco. She let her cry on her shoulder, and gave her words of advice. Promising her that we would find out who did this, and murder their whole fuckin' family, I let a tear fall down my face to show a little compassion, but I knew this was something I would be definitely taking with me to my grave.

"Listen, Coco. I'm really sorry for what happened, but we have to leave her and get outta here. After everything that's happened, and all the shots that's been fired, I'm surprised the police haven't shown up yet," Mahogany said, hugging Coco as she cried her heart out.

After about five minutes, Coco finally stood to her feet, and pulled Shanel's body out of the car. "Rest in peace, baby, and until we meet again, I want you to know that I love you," she said before kissing her on the forehead. We all said our last goodbyes and then pulled off like a thief in the night.

It was ten o'clock the next morning when I woke up to the news broadcasting what they called the homicide of the year.

"I'm Brittany Collins, bringing you the latest of the St. Petersburg massacre. We have now been informed that seven bodies have been found with gunshot wounds to the head or chest, which is the cause of death. None of the bodies have been identified due to the ongoing investigation, and the way the murder took place, detectives are saying it had to be the work of professional killers, which belong to the mob. This is the biggest tragedy that's taken place in St. Petersburg this year, and on the behalf of all the mothers, fathers, sisters, brothers, and children who've lost a loved one yesterday, we would like to have a moment of silence to remember them." She took the mic away from her mouth, and then closed her eyes before bowing her head.

The camera man was still recording as Brittany Collins did her job, and lied to the world, like she really cared about the people who were killed. To me that was flawed as fuck, but hey, who am I to judge?

"Ladies and gentlemen, that was all the news for now, but we will be sure to bring you the updates as they come. So, stay tuned and remember, you heard it here first. I'm Brittany Collins, and this is CFTNS."

I turned off the TV, then went to get in the shower. I felt so dirty in the skin I was in, I mean, it felt tainted. I couldn't believe I'd turned into a killer. What kind of person would enjoy taking another person's life, I thought as I undressed, and stepped under the shower head. I let the steaming water caress my body and relaxed as my worries went away. I was living carefree at the moment, and wished it would last for a lifetime. Water started falling down my face, but as my eyes started to sting, I realized it wasn't from the shower head. I was crying, and didn't even know what I was crying about until my thoughts went wild, and I started thinking about Nah Nah, Nicole, and Shanel. I was crying for them, because their lives ended too early, because they would never get to enjoy the experience of motherhood, and their family and friends would never have a chance to see their beautiful faces again.

Life was crazy, and the bad thing about it, you had no control over the hand you'd been dealt. Like they say, God has already planned your life, and the struggles you would face before you're even out of your mother's womb. I feel like that's fucked up, because before I'm even born, it's already destined that I could die before I'm two months old. Damn!

I got out of the shower after about ten more minutes, dried off, and got dressed before I walked downstairs. The house felt different without Nah Nah, Nicole, and Shanel. It felt empty. I continued to the kitchen to fix myself a cup of coffee and all of a sudden, I started missing my mother. It had been a while since I'd talked to her. Come to think about it, more like three months. My mother was a sweet woman with a big heart, and I knew things hadn't been easy for her since my father had died. But I continued to make it hard for her, like the way I treated her in her house, when all she did was try to take care of me when I got shot.

I needed to apologize, because the way this world's going, tomorrow was not promised, and I couldn't live with myself if my mother left this earth without her knowing how I really felt.

"Hello, this is the Newman's residence. How may I help you?" my mother answered on the third ring. 'She sounded like she was in a good mood, and I was happy to hear that she was still alive at least.

"Ma, this is E'mani. You don't have to talk all proper when I call," I greeted her with an upbeat voice. She inhaled taking a deep breath as if she was shocked that I called, then replied,

"Baby, I'm so glad you called. Are you alright? I had a dream a couple days ago that you were arrested for murder. I woke up and prayed until I couldn't stop the tears from falling down my face, but God told me that you have to come to Him yourself, and ask for forgiveness. Baby, I don't know what's been going on in your life, but you need to start praying, and coming back to church."

"Ma, I'm fine, and stop believing what you see in your dreams, because they are not real. That's why they're called dreams, but Ma, I know everything hasn't been peaches and cream between you and me since Daddy died, and I want to say sorry. Sorry for how I treated you the last time we were together and sorry for not being the daughter I once was. I love you." I opened up to her. I really did love my mother, and meant every word I'd said. So after we talked for about twenty more minutes, I hung up, still feeling like the world was about to end.

## Chapter Twenty-Six
### Mahogany

Ever since I was twelve years old, my life had been hell so the devil basically raised me. I mean, don't get me wrong, there had been some good times, but overall, I'd always ended up with the shit end of the deal throughout my life. I stood in my room directly in front of my mirror surveying every inch of my body. I wanted to know what the fuck I did wrong, to end up with a life like mine. I had a flawless body, a million-dollar smile, and a brain as if I had a master's degree in science.

I blamed it all on my mother. It was because of her that God didn't love me. It was because of her I grew up poor, and it was because of her that I didn't have the childhood of most little girls.

I got dressed after about five minutes, because today was going to be a long day. It had been two weeks since that shit went down with Ja'mya and Kayla and so far, I was glad our names hadn't been mentioned. But today, we were laying our girls down to rest. Yeah, it was Nah Nah, Nicole, and Shanel's funeral. We made all of the arrangements and even called their families to attend, but like it or not, they were getting buried right here in St. Pete.

After I checked myself in the mirror one last time, I shielded my eyes with my RayBan shades, and headed downstairs. E'mani and Coco were still getting ready, so I took this time to collect my thoughts. We still had to go through all of Nah Nah, Nicole, and Shanel's things, which nobody even made an attempt to do. It was hard, knowing I wouldn't be able to see my girls anymore, and going into their rooms now would only make things more complicated. I peeped out the window, seeing that the limo was here, and then yelled upstairs to Coco and E'mani before making my way outside.

Inside the limo, we all sat quiet as we rode to the church. I was reminiscing, and trying to think about all the good times we'd shared, like the time we did our thing in Deland at Club Paid, and I was about to give Hollywood his red wings. He tried to get gangsta on a bitch, but Nah Nah was right there like the Grim Reaper, almost causing him to shit on himself. I smiled, thinking about how my girl Nah Nah always had our backs no matter what. Damn, I miss her already.

What about the time Coco rolled up a blunt of loud and laced it with Molly? Yeah, that shit had Nicole trippin', runnin' around in public in her panties and bra, yelling that I was trying to kill her. I can laugh about it now, but at the time, my girl was really fighting some demons. And then the time we were at the Florida Institution for Teenage Girls, and Shanel got into a fight with this big gorilla bitch named Robbin. Robbin had stolen some pictures of Shanel's boyfriend Trey, and went around telling people that it was her man. Shanel caught her while she was on the phone talking to her family, and beat her ass with a lock in a sock. By the time we got there, Shanel was talking to Robbin's people, and telling them why she had just got her ass beat with a lock.

There were so many good memories we all shared, and now, we would never get the chance to sit around, and tell our children and it hurt. I saw E'mani and Coco looking at me, and I tried to blink back my tears, but it was no use. They were flowing like a flood in a city. "You're thinking about them right now and trying to hold back your tears, but you don't have to be strong for us. Just let it all out, girl," Coco said moving closer to me before we embraced in a big bear hug like loving sisters. I really needed that hug, but I was pissed off at myself for letting them see me cry. I was the strong one, the one that they all looked up to, and now I was breaking down like an old station wagon.

We pulled up to the church, and I fixed myself before exiting the limo. I couldn't believe all the people I saw when I stepped inside. There were people I knew and then there were people I didn't know if I knew. Nah Nah's mother found me, and we got to talking as if we'd known each other for years until reality settled in, and I gave her my shoulder to cry on. I explained to her that everything would be alright, but how can you convince a mother who had just lost her child that everything was alright? It's sad that I didn't see any of Nicole's family. I knew she had grown up in and out of group homes, but damn, was all I could say. It didn't get me upset though, because through thick and thin, I was always there for my girls, and today was no different. I waved and smiled as I saw Coco talking to her mother, but the way her eyes were all puffy and red, I could tell she had been crying.

Reverend Coleman found me as I was about to take my seat to give me a few words of encouragement. "Mahogany, I am so sorry for your loss, and it hurt me to my heart to see the bodies of these three young ladies here right now, but it was God's plan, and there is nothing anyone of us could have done to save them. I could see in your eyes that you're grieving, but please do not blame yourself for what happened to these young ladies." I took what he'd said into consideration, but how could I sit here, and not blame myself for what happened to them? It was I who took from Supreme, and it was I who caused the war, so why wouldn't I feel like it was my fault?

The reverend found his way to the podium and cleared his throat, before starting with his sermon. "Ladies and gentlemen, we are gathered here today to celebrate the homecoming of three beautiful young ladies. Notice that I said homecoming and not the funeral, because God has called them home to live an everlasting life in Heaven with Him. What's not to celebrate about that?"

"Amen! Tell 'em, Reverend," a woman yelled out. Reverend Coleman smiled before eying a couple women, and then continued.

"I never had the pleasure of meeting these three ladies, but I was told that Heaven would never see a smile upside down, because their spirits were one of a child who woke up on Christmas Day to find every toy she'd asked of Santa." Everybody laughed at the reverend's sense of humor, and even I caught myself smiling from time to time.

"I would like to call another young lady who actually grew up with and knew the three ladies on a personal side. I know right now she might not want all the attention on her, but I feel this would be a good time to share with everybody the good nature of the girls. Ladies and gentlemen, Miss Mahogany."

I looked around as everybody clapped, but didn't actually get up from my seat until E'mani grabbed my arm, forcing me up. I nervously walked towards the reverend, and gave him a hug before watching him take his seat. I didn't expect this, and God knows I didn't know what I was going to say. Everybody could tell I was nervous, and to give me a little encouragement, I heard somebody yell, "Take your time, baby. We all know how hard it is."

I tried to smile, but the tears had returned before I knew it. "Would you all please excuse my tears, because everything has come as a big surprise to me? Now I could stand here and say all of these good things about the girls, and how they never did wrong, but that would be a lie. They were far from being saints, but they all had hearts, believed in helping others and they made a way of leaving a special feeling in anybody they came across. I've been through so much with them that blood couldn't make us any closer to being family than we already are." This was really not me. Mahogany don't speak in front of crowds of people, but I continued until I just didn't have anything else to say. I looked at E'mani and Coco for help, but they both gave me a look that said I better not call their names to speak. Reverend Coleman took the podium, saving me, and ending with a prayer that really touched me. We all rode to the burial site and cried once again as they lowered the girls in the ground, right next to each other. I would never forget my girls. It's Baller Babies for life, and a bitch better not forget that.

Everybody came back to our house to eat and relax. I was glad, because my feet were starting to hurt in these darn heels and my pinky toe was screaming for help. Once I went to my room to change into something a little more comfortable, I made my way back downstairs to mingle with our guests. Coco, E'mani nor I cooked that well, so we had to order from this soul food joint and to my surprise, nobody even knew the difference. I walked around making sure everybody was comfortable, even though under these circumstances, it was kind of hard. Some people were still crying and grieving, while others enjoyed themselves by the pool and basketball court. E'mani and Coco found me as I walked out to the pool area or should I say, I found them, because they both were relaxing with their feet in the water.

"Having fun?" I asked, smiling like I had just shined my gold teeth.

"Girl, I'm just trying to get past everything that's been going on. I can't believe what happened, but today is a new day and with the life we were living, shit like that is expected. I just hate it had to happen to the Baller Babies," Coco said, shaking her head. I agreed with her about life going on and right now, I didn't have any more tears. I was all cried out. It was time to have some fun, and cheer up. That's why what I had planned for the Baller Babies would never be forgotten.

"Cheer up, girl, because I have a surprise for y'all. Tonight just make sure your shit is on fleek, because we turnin' up to the damn max." I let what I said sink in, then turned on the heels of my feet to kick everybody who didn't live here out of my damn house. Was I wrong for that?

"Attention to all the real niggas, go-getters, bad bitches, and show stoppers. We got some hood stars that just walked into the building, and if your timing ain't right or you ain't on fleek tonight, then you need to get the fuck out. It ain't my B-day, but everybody need to open their mouth, and shout out them mutha-fuckin' Baller Babies." The whole club went crazy as my big dawg DJ Red Eyes introduced us. Coco, E'mani, and I sashayed through the club like the bad bitches we were. I couldn't front, it was some fly bitches everywhere I looked, but the one-piece cat suits personally made by the collaboration of Tom Ford, and Shanel had the Baller Babies
looking like royalty. Yeah, this was our night, and we were about to turn this bitch out.

Red Eyes kept playing some of the hottest of the hottest throwback joints, like Mariah Carey's "We Belong Together," Rihanna's "Work," and Beyoncé's "Flawless," "Drunk In Love" and "Sorry." I can't lie, I was fucked up about Beyoncé. That's my girl, and whoever Becky with the good hair was, she should've

191

beat that bitch's ass after kicking Jay Z's ass to the curb. But then again, she brought that on herself, because knowing black men can't keep their dicks in their pants, she was the one that told him if he liked it, then he should've put a ring on it.

We had our own section on the right side of the club, and our table was blessed with every popular bottle of liquor you could name. Rémy, VSOP, Grey Goose, Cîroc, and Rosé, just to name a few. We weren't in VIP, but the way we hung out, you would've thought we were.

"Mahogany, girl, this what I'm talking about. They sweatin' us like we're celebrities in this bitch. A bitch can get used to this," Coco shouted over the music. I could tell E'mani was having a good time too, the way she was throwing her ass on the dance floor between two men that made me smile. After all the stressing we'd been doing, this was a long overdue celebration.

"Double B's, bitch!" I shouted, just for the hell of it.

We all got on the dance floor doin' our thing, but I would be lying if I said the hard dicks I was grinding on wasn't turning me on. If my cat suit wasn't so tight, I would've whipped out a condom and bent over bustin' this pussy open from the back, no lie. After a while, we went back to our table, and I swear I felt like a don diva, the way so many people stepped to us asking if they could get a chance to prove themselves to become a Baller Baby, after apologizing for our loss, men included. I didn't think we were ready to start recruiting people to take Nah Nah, Nicole or Shanel's place, so we took their names and numbers before telling them we would keep in touch.

It was six thirty in the morning when we left the club and by the time we made it to the house, the sun was just starting to rise. It had been a while since I stayed out this late and I was starting to get too old for it. We all stumbled into the house, trying to get to our beds, but the minute we reached the staircase we were stopped by loud banging, as if somebody was trying to beat our door down. We waited to see who the muthafucka was banging like the police, while E'mani went to answer it. Once she opened it, all signs of intoxication left our bodies, well at least mine.

"Emani Newman. You are under arrest for accessory to the murder of Jermain 'Supreme' Waltson," one of the officers said as they placed cuffs on E'mani's wrists. I wanted to scream, but it surprised me the way E'mani was handling the situation before mouthing two names, Ashlyn and Alice. I looked at Coco, not knowing what to do next. I really couldn't understand what the hell was going on. Why were they locking E'mani up for being accessory to Supreme's murder when we all knew that Hollywood murked him? We continued to stare as they put E'mani in the backseat before driving off.

"What the fuuuuuuck! I hate these fuckin' pigs," I shouted as I slammed the front door and cried as another one of my sista's had to fight to not get lost in the fuckin' system. This year had been one hell of a year and one thing I can say is that I would never forget it. We didn't know what they would do with E'mani, but one thing I did know was that I had to hold my bitch down and stand in the paint, no matter what her bid would be. Believe that!

## "Coco"

I secretly laughed as Mahogany cried while they took E'mani's backstabbin' ass to jail. One thing I'd learned in my young life of living was that karma is a dirty ass bitch and she will come when you least expect it. To everybody who thinks I don't know what the fuck is going on, you are dumb bitches and you can eat my pussy. It's like this. When you have a twin, you know when something's not right with them. You know when they're hurt, you know when they cry and you know when they're feeling like they're on top of the world. It's a feeling you get that can't be described in words, something you feel in your soul because you're feeling it, as if it's happening to you.

I know E'mani killed my sister. I felt it the day it happened. I just didn't want to believe it. Then my sister spoke to my soul, which had never happened to me before, and it became clear that's why E'mani kept dodging me. It hurts so bad to witness my mother cry over the loss of her child and I couldn't do anything about it. I will get my revenge even if it takes days, months or years. E'mani's ass is mine. Long live the double fuckin' B's, bitch!

"E'mani"

"I'm locked up. They won't let me out!" I sung in the voice of Akon as I tried to downplay my situation, but truth be told, I was about to lose my mind. I didn't think my life could get fucked up any more than what it was until I found myself in the back seat of a police car. I'm pretty sure Ashlyn and Alice dropped a dime on me, but then again, it could have been anybody. I didn't know who the fuck to trust no more. I had always thought of my girls as having my back, but loyalty ain't shit. Look how Kayla flipped on us, and then what about Supreme? I thought he was in love with me because that's what he told me every time he ate my kitty, but I guess he really wasn't, because I could see clear as day that Mahogany had his heart. Neeko tricked me while he played up under me, and even Shanel was a backstabber. I was starting to feel like Pac and believe it really was me against the world.

I tried to pray, something I hadn't done in a while, but I didn't think God would hear me from all the times I'd lied to him. Once that didn't work out, I started to think about my life and where it was headed. Mama was going to have a heart attack and it was eating me up inside how much I was taking her through.

When I finally made it to the county jail and went through the process of intake, I felt like I lost all will to fight. I just wanted to get this shit over with. Once I did see the judge, he denied me a bond, which ripped my heart into a million pieces and then I was taken to the second floor where I was being housed. Soon as I stepped foot in my housing unit, all I saw was red and I took off, swinging as if my life depended on it. I wasn't fighting to survive or because I wanted to make a statement. I was fighting because revenge was bittersweet and I had finally caught my victim's ass out and with no panties on. While I was beating her ass like a mother who'd caught her daughter stealing her rent money, all I could hear was women screaming at the top of their lungs. "Ashlyn! Beat that bitch's ass. Beat her ass good girl!" Then, I saw darkness.

*To Be Continued...*
Loyalty Ain't Promised 2
Coming Soon

# Submission Guideline

Submit the first three chapters of your completed manuscript to ldpsubmissions@gmail.com, subject line: Your book's title. The manuscript must be in a .doc file and sent as an attachment. Document should be in Times New Roman, double spaced and in size 12 font. Also, provide your synopsis and full contact information. If sending multiple submissions, they must each be in a separate email.

Have a story but no way to send it electronically? You can still submit to LDP/Ca$h Presents. Send in the first three chapters, written or typed, of your completed manuscript to:

**LDP: Submissions Dept**
**Po Box 870494**
**Mesquite, Tx 75187**

*DO NOT send original manuscript. Must be a duplicate.*

Provide your synopsis and a cover letter containing your full contact information.

Thanks for considering LDP and Ca$h Presents.

**Coming Soon from Lock Down Publications/Ca$h Presents**

BOW DOWN TO MY GANGSTA

By **Ca$h**

TORN BETWEEN TWO

By **Coffee**

THE STREETS STAINED MY SOUL **II**

By **Marcellus Allen**

BLOOD OF A BOSS **VI**

SHADOWS OF THE GAME II

By **Askari**

LOYAL TO THE GAME **IV**

By **T.J. & Jelissa**

A DOPEBOY'S PRAYER **II**

By **Eddie "Wolf" Lee**

IF LOVING YOU IS WRONG… **III**

By **Jelissa**

TRUE SAVAGE **VII**

MIDNIGHT CARTEL III

DOPE BOY MAGIC III

By **Chris Green**

BLAST FOR ME **III**

DUFFLE BAG CARTEL **IV**

A SAVAGE DOPEBOY III

By **Ghost**

A HUSTLER'S DECEIT III

KILL ZONE **II**

BAE BELONGS TO ME III

SOUL OF A MONSTER III

By **Aryanna**

THE COST OF LOYALTY **III**

By **Kweli**

CHAINED TO THE STREETS II

By **J-Blunt**

KING OF NEW YORK V

COKE KINGS IV

BORN HEARTLESS IV

By **T.J. Edwards**

GORILLAZ IN THE BAY V

**De'Kari**

THE STREETS ARE CALLING II

**Duquie Wilson**

KINGPIN KILLAZ IV

STREET KINGS III

PAID IN BLOOD III

CARTEL KILLAZ IV

**Hood Rich**

SINS OF A HUSTLA II

**ASAD**

TRIGGADALE III

**Elijah R. Freeman**

KINGZ OF THE GAME V

**Playa Ray**

SLAUGHTER GANG IV

RUTHLESS HEART III

**By Willie Slaughter**

THE HEART OF A SAVAGE II

**By Jibril Williams**

FUK SHYT II

**By Blakk Diamond**

THE DOPEMAN'S BODYGAURD II

**By Tranay Adams**

TRAP GOD II

**By Troublesome**

YAYO III

A SHOOTER'S AMBITION II

**By S. Allen**

GHOST MOB

**Stilloan Robinson**

KINGPIN DREAMS II

**By Paper Boi Rari**

CREAM

**By Yolanda Moore**

SON OF A DOPE FIEND II

**By Renta**

FOREVER GANGSTA II

**By Adrian Dulan**

LOYALTY AIN'T PROMISED II

**By Keith Williams**

THE PRICE YOU PAY FOR LOVE II

**By Destiny Skai**

THE LIFE OF A HOOD STAR

**By Rashia Wilson**

TOE TAGZ III

**By Ah'Million**

CONFESSIONS OF A GANGSTA II

**By Nicholas Lock**

PAID IN KARMA II

By **Meesha**

I'M NOTHING WITHOUT HIS LOVE II

**By Monet Dragun**
CAUGHT UP IN THE LIFE II
**By Robert Baptiste**
NEW TO THE GAME II
By **Malik D. Rice**
Life of a Savage II
By **Romell Tukes**

## Available Now

RESTRAINING ORDER **I & II**
By **CA$H & Coffee**
LOVE KNOWS NO BOUNDARIES **I II & III**
By **Coffee**
RAISED AS A GOON I, II,  III & IV
BRED BY THE SLUMS I, II, III
BLAST FOR ME I & II
ROTTEN TO THE CORE I II III
A BRONX TALE I, II, III
DUFFEL BAG CARTEL I II III
HEARTLESS GOON I II III IV
A SAVAGE DOPEBOY I II
HEARTLESS GOON I II III
DRUG LORDS I II III
By **Ghost**
LAY IT DOWN **I & II**
LAST OF A DYING BREED
BLOOD STAINS OF A SHOTTA I & II III
By **Jamaica**

## Loyalty Ain't Promised

LOYAL TO THE GAME I II III

LIFE OF SIN I, II III

By **TJ & Jelissa**

BLOODY COMMAS I & II

SKI MASK CARTEL I II & III

KING OF NEW YORK I II,III IV

RISE TO POWER I II III

COKE KINGS I II III

BORN HEARTLESS I II III

By **T.J. Edwards**

IF LOVING HIM IS WRONG…I & II

LOVE ME EVEN WHEN IT HURTS I II III

By **Jelissa**

WHEN THE STREETS CLAP BACK I & II III

By **Jibril Williams**

A DISTINGUISHED THUG STOLE MY HEART I II & III

LOVE SHOULDN'T HURT I II III IV

RENEGADE BOYS I II III IV

PAID IN KARMA

By **Meesha**

A GANGSTER'S CODE I &, II III

A GANGSTER'S SYN I II III

THE SAVAGE LIFE I II III

CHAINED TO THE STREETS

By **J-Blunt**

PUSH IT TO THE LIMIT

By **Bre' Hayes**

BLOOD OF A BOSS **I, II, III, IV, V**

SHADOWS OF THE GAME

By **Askari**

THE STREETS BLEED MURDER **I, II & III**

THE HEART OF A GANGSTA I II& III

By **Jerry Jackson**

CUM FOR ME I II III IV V

An **LDP Erotica Collaboration**

BRIDE OF A HUSTLA **I  II & II**

THE FETTI GIRLS **I, II& III**

CORRUPTED BY A GANGSTA I, II III, IV

BLINDED BY HIS LOVE

THE PRICE YOU PAY FOR LOVE

By **Destiny Skai**

WHEN A GOOD GIRL GOES BAD

By **Adrienne**

THE COST OF LOYALTY I II

**By Kweli**

A GANGSTER'S REVENGE **I II III & IV**

THE BOSS MAN'S DAUGHTERS I II III IV V

A SAVAGE LOVE **I & II**

BAE BELONGS TO ME I II

A HUSTLER'S DECEIT I, II, III

WHAT BAD BITCHES DO I, II, III

SOUL OF A MONSTER I II

KILL ZONE

By **Aryanna**

A KINGPIN'S AMBITON

A KINGPIN'S AMBITION **II**

I MURDER FOR THE DOUGH

By **Ambitious**

TRUE SAVAGE I II III IV V VI

DOPE BOY MAGIC I, II

## Loyalty Ain't Promised

MIDNIGHT CARTEL I II

By **Chris Green**

A DOPEBOY'S PRAYER

By **Eddie "Wolf" Lee**

THE KING CARTEL **I, II & III**

By **Frank Gresham**

THESE NIGGAS AIN'T LOYAL **I, II & III**

By **Nikki Tee**

GANGSTA SHYT **I II &III**

By **CATO**

THE ULTIMATE BETRAYAL

By **Phoenix**

BOSS'N UP **I , II & III**

By **Royal Nicole**

I LOVE YOU TO DEATH

**By Destiny J**

I RIDE FOR MY HITTA

I STILL RIDE FOR MY HITTA

By **Misty Holt**

LOVE & CHASIN' PAPER

By **Qay Crockett**

TO DIE IN VAIN

SINS OF A HUSTLA

By **ASAD**

BROOKLYN HUSTLAZ

By **Boogsy Morina**

BROOKLYN ON LOCK I & II

By **Sonovia**

GANGSTA CITY

By **Teddy Duke**

Keith Williams

A DRUG KING AND HIS DIAMOND I & II III
A DOPEMAN'S RICHES
HER MAN, MINE'S TOO I, II
CASH MONEY HO'S
**By Nicole Goosby**
TRAPHOUSE KING **I II & III**
KINGPIN KILLAZ I II III
STREET KINGS I II
PAID IN BLOOD **I II**
CARTEL KILLAZ I II III
By **Hood Rich**
LIPSTICK KILLAH **I, II, III**
CRIME OF PASSION I II & III
By **Mimi**
STEADY MOBBN' **I, II, III**
THE STREETS STAINED MY SOUL
By **Marcellus Allen**
WHO SHOT YA **I, II, III**
SON OF A DOPE FIEND
**Renta**
GORILLAZ IN THE BAY **I II III IV**
**DE'KARI**
TRIGGADALE I II
**Elijah R. Freeman**
GOD BLESS THE TRAPPERS I, II, III
THESE SCANDALOUS STREETS I, II, III
FEAR MY GANGSTA I, II, III
THESE STREETS DON'T LOVE NOBODY I, II
BURY ME A G I, II, III, IV, V
A GANGSTA'S EMPIRE I, II, III, IV

THE DOPEMAN'S BODYGAURD

**Tranay Adams**

THE STREETS ARE CALLING

**Duquie Wilson**

MARRIED TO A BOSS... I II III

**By Destiny Skai & Chris Green**

KINGZ OF THE GAME I  II III IV

**Playa Ray**

SLAUGHTER GANG I II III

RUTHLESS HEART I II

**By Willie Slaughter**

THE HEART OF A SAVAGE

**By Jibril Williams**

FUK SHYT

**By Blakk Diamond**

DON'T F#CK WITH MY HEART I II

**By Linnea**

ADDICTED TO THE DRAMA I II III

**By Jamila**

YAYO I II

A SHOOTER'S AMBITION

**By S. Allen**

TRAP GOD

**By Troublesome**

FOREVER GANGSTA

**By Adrian Dulan**

TOE TAGZ I II

**By Ah'Million**

KINGPIN DREAMS

**By Paper Boi Rari**

CONFESSIONS OF A GANGSTA

**By Nicholas Lock**

I'M NOTHING WITHOUT HIS LOVE

**By Monet Dragun**

CAUGHT UP IN THE LIFE

**By Robert Baptiste**

NEW TO THE GAME

By **Malik D. Rice**

Life of a Savage

By **Romell Tukes**

LOYALTY AIN'T PROMISED

**By Keith Williams**

**<u>BOOKS BY LDP'S CEO, CA$H</u>**

<u>TRUST IN NO MAN</u>
<u>TRUST IN NO MAN 2</u>
<u>TRUST IN NO MAN 3</u>
<u>BONDED BY BLOOD</u>
<u>SHORTY GOT A THUG</u>
<u>THUGS CRY</u>
<u>THUGS CRY 2</u>
<u>THUGS CRY 3</u>
<u>TRUST NO BITCH</u>
<u>TRUST NO BITCH 2</u>
<u>TRUST NO BITCH 3</u>
<u>TIL MY CASKET DROPS</u>
<u>RESTRAINING ORDER</u>
<u>RESTRAINING ORDER 2</u>
<u>IN LOVE WITH A CONVICT</u>

**<u>Coming Soon</u>**
BONDED BY BLOOD 2
BOW DOWN TO MY GANGSTA

Keith Williams